DIRTY MONEY

DIRTY
MONEY

Ray Russell

_____

ST. MARTIN'S PRESS

NEW YORK

Library of Congress Cataloging-in-Publication Data

Russell, Ray.
    Dirty money / by Ray Russell.
        p.   cm.
    ISBN 0–312–01368–X : $15.95
    I. Title.
PS3568.U77D5   1988
813'.54—dc19   87–27334

First Edition

10 9 8 7 6 5 4 3 2 1

To my wife
ADA BETH
in gratitude

DIRTY MONEY

Part

I

1

"**U**P and at 'em," he muttered to himself. "Today is the first day of the rest of the week."

The desert sun of late morning had dazzled him into waking, and he'd phoned down for a breakfast of orange juice, sunnyside eggs, sausages, buckwheat cakes, syrup, rye toast, coffee, and a newspaper. He believed in keeping up his strength. Some people he knew ate awful stuff for breakfast. Like granola, or muesli—that was the same as eating carpenter's shavings! Suicide! Terrible way to start a day.

While he waited for breakfast, he took stock of his life.

He wasn't getting any younger. If he squinted real hard and shaded his eyes, he could see middle age smirking at him a few years down the road. Forty! He shook his head in dismay and disbelief. He had hated his thirtieth birthday, and he knew he would absolutely loathe and detest his fortieth.

His "career"—to dignify it by the word—had been spinning its wheels in the same mud for years.

Tomorrow could make a lot of difference. He had a chance at a big score. If he pulled it off in the way that was expected of him—in the way he expected of himself—he might just lift himself up by his bootstraps, right up out of the rut he'd been stuck in for much too long. If he bungled it, he'd become a back number quicker than the Susan B.

Anthony dollar. But he wouldn't bungle it. He couldn't. Too much depended on it.

His order arrived. For the moment, he was content to stay in his air-conditioned room, propped up in bed, eating, sipping coffee, turning the pages of the newspaper. He drifted into sleep again, more tired than he had realized, a convalescent needing rest, recuperating from the stresses and risks of his last assignment. When he awoke again, he was surprised to see that the room was ink-blue-and-old-brass with twilight. He sprang out of bed, blasted his body with an icy shower, dressed, and left the hotel.

The city was brilliantly ugly. The sky itself was stained with an artificial aurora borealis. If the great egomaniac kings of old had known about neon, this is the way their tombs and monuments may have looked—pulsing, sizzling, clashing with color, searing the eye and dizzying the mind—Sphinx and pyramids and frowning Ozymandias bleaching the ancient heavens with throbbing light designed to be seen from the Moon and to shame that rival god, the Sun.

Damn good thing they *hadn't* known about neon.

He wandered along the Strip, awed and appalled, ingesting the bad taste, gorging it like junk food. Far off on the horizon there was beauty—the city was ringed by mountains, black in the dying sunlight—but these natural beauties interested him less than the flashing electric lights, taller than King Kong, spelling out the names of singers and comics and glossy sequined sexpots of the screen. It was his first visit to Las Vegas. Also his last, he hoped.

He moved as in an endless dream, in and out of Caesars Palace, where the togas were as stiff and white as porcelain, and the MGM, where the plush was as deeply red as dried blood, and the soothing blue of the Tropicana, and the Hilton, where the chandeliers looked like the

4

diamond headdresses of some towering imperial race of giants.

He journeyed into the city's downtown section, Glitter Gulch, roamed through the Golden Nugget, the Four Queens, the Mint, the Horseshoe. He fed coins into slot machines, standing next to leathery matrons, hearing them squeal and shriek, the sounds frying his ears. Most of them were as old as his mother, or older.

The machines, many of them video poker and blackjack slots, were aligned not in the old traditional straight rows but in circular patterns, contributing to the calculated psychological effect of frenzy. The dollar machines were equipped with aluminum trays that created the loudest possible clatter when the coins spilled into them, making a twenty-dollar win sound like a fortune.

He walked from game to game, from table to table, from casino to hotel to casino. Blackjack, baccarat, roulette, crap, even the names crackled with cacophony, like dragging a stick along a picket fence. . . .

But out of the turmoil, his first night in Vegas, Lady Luck dealt him the Queen of Hearts.

The flaming red corona of her hair had something to do with it; the sea green of her eyes; the gloss of near-nude flesh; high pink domes of breasts; Cyclopean navel; long curves of thighs and calves; the ample, glistening mouth; but these were merely the multiple magnets that first attracted his senses. Something else, he told himself, an indefinable other element, singled her out from the rest of the knockouts in the chorus line; a thick bright spark that hissed and writhed between the pair of them, two human electrodes in mad Frankenstein's lab; an affinity, a mutuality, a recognition, good vibes . . .

He caught himself just in time, before he labeled the feeling Love.

Whew! That was a close one!

But he waited for her, after the last show, at a drab rear

5

exit of the club. When he saw her come out, in pants, flat shoes, red hair wrapped in a scarf, minus that comic-book queen-of-the-vampires eye makeup, he fell into step beside her. She looked up at him with suspicion.

"Buy you a cup of coffee?" he offered.

"Who the hell are *you*?"

"I saw you in there. You saw me, too."

"I see a million guys. A million guys see me."

"But I felt something."

"I bet you *did*."

"No, not like that. I mean, something special. You felt it, too. I could tell."

"I smile at *all* the customers, mister. It's called show business."

"This hard-nose routine of yours," he said, "*that's* show business. It's not the real you. I can read people. I have to, in my business. And I can tell you're not as cheap as you pretend to be. So how about that cup of coffee?"

He wasn't bad looking. She favored him with a grudging half-smile. "That's some line you've got. All right, one cup. Decaffeinated."

In the all-night coffeeshop across the street, over decaf and Jell-O salad, she was saying, "So what line of business are you in, anyway?"

"It's . . . highly sensitive," he said. "I can't talk about it. Not until I know you a lot better."

"Secret stuff, huh?"

"That's right. But tomorrow I'll be making a big score . . ."

"At the tables, is that it?" she said with a mixture of pity and contempt. "Listen, this city was *built* on the hopes of suckers like you. Forget it."

"No, no, not gambling. Business. And if I score big enough tomorrow, I may be able to get into a branch of my business that's a lot better. Safer, more money, less . . ."

"Less 'highly sensitive'?"

"Close enough. And I want you to come with me . . . back east."

"*Me?* You don't even *know* me!"

"I told you. I can read people. And I know that behind all that hardcase act and that great body that you flash half naked up there on that stage, you're a good kid, someone I've got things in common with. I feel it."

"*I* feel you're some kind of flake."

"I can live with that for now. Will you have breakfast with me tomorrow?"

"I don't know. Maybe . . ."

"Where do you live? I'll pick you up."

"No, thanks," she said cautiously. "I'll meet you here. But I sleep late. Make it eleven and call it brunch."

"Deal."

As soon as the post office opened the next morning, he was inside, headed for the p.o. box. Opening it, he plucked out a large brown envelope, bulging with its contents, and quickly left the building, stuffing the envelope into an inner pocket.

He slipped quietly inside the nearest available men's room, locked himself in a booth, and ripped the fat envelope open. Into his hand tumbled a wad of cash as thick as a club sandwich. Fifty thousand dollars. He didn't have to count it. Next came an index card with a name and address typed on it. Also two photographs, front view and profile.

His mouth fell open.

The face in the photos had hit him with a shock, an unpleasant surprise. But, in another way, it was perfect. It provided him with a ready-made excuse to play for time.

He had to get to a phone. But not out where everybody and his brother could overhear him. Finally he found one at a self-service filling station doing no business at that moment. He dialed the safe number, waited impatiently

7

through four rings, then heard a calm male voice say, "Yes?"

"We've got to talk," he said.

"Who's this?"

"Jersey."

"You got a problem, Jersey?"

"Listen, I just picked up the package."

"So? Do your job and get out of town. The money's right, isn't it? The other fifty will be sent to your other p.o. box when you get back to Newark. Half now, half later, like we said."

"I don't hit broads."

"What?"

"You never told me it was a broad. I didn't know it until I saw the name and the photos. And I don't hit broads. Everyone knows that."

"I don't know that! And Mr. R don't know that! Are you crazy enough to go sour on a deal with *him?"*

A silver Topaz rolled into the filling station and the driver climbed out to fill his tank. Jersey was obliged to whisper: "Why does Mr. R want her hit?"

"That's none of your business. Just do the job you were hired for and hop that noon flight out of here. If you *don't* . . ." The unspoken threat hung in the air like a bad smell. There was a jolting click and a hum, and he was standing there holding a dead telephone.

It was ten o'clock. He caught a cab and went straight to her apartment.

Opening the door to his insistent knock, her green eyes narrowed as she said, "How did you find me?" She was still in her robe. "And I thought we said eleven."

He pushed his way in. "Just listen. Why does Big Sally Rich want you killed?"

"Who?"

"Don't play dumb. If I know what we're up against,

maybe I can save you. Why is Big Sally paying me a hundred grand to put your lights out?"

She looked at him closely. "That's your top-secret business? *I'm* your big score?" He nodded. "You're serious, aren't you?" she said.

"You're damn right I'm serious, lady!" He slapped the envelope into her hand. "I picked that up this morning. The front half of my fee and the name and address of my contract. Plus a couple of mug shots. Not very flattering, but recognizable. Take a look."

She slid the contents out of the envelope and examined them, pushing red hair away from her eyes. "That's me, all right," she admitted. More to herself than to him, she added, "Then Sally knows. He's even smarter than I thought." Briskly, she said, "Now let me get this straight. Are you trying to tell me that you've been hired by Salvatore Ricci to murder me?"

"That's right," he said. "A hundred-G score. And I want to know *why*. Why are you worth that much to him dead?"

"Well," she said, pulling a short, flat .380 Browning automatic from her robe pocket, "maybe because I've got the goods on him, and he knows it. And now I've got the goods on you, too."

"What are you talking about? Who *are* you?"

"Field Investigator Kittering," she replied. "Justice Department. And you are under arrest, Mr. Hit Man."

He laughed. "I don't believe it. *You* . . . you're Federal?"

She flashed her I.D. "I strung you along last night because all your talk about a big score and highly sensitive business deals made me suspect you might be a dope dealer. I never figured on bagging a hired gun." He was still laughing. "Go ahead and laugh," she said. "But the laugh is on you."

He sat down, his knees weak from laughter. "Not only on me," he said.

2

"**M**R. R don't like this," the owner of the telephone voice said darkly when Jersey arrived at the Ricci house.

"Oh, no?" said Jersey.

"No." The owner of the voice was a thick man, and swarthy, as thick and swarthy as his voice, with skin the texture of cold gravy. "Mr. R," he added, "never deals personally with people like you."

"This time he will, I think."

"Maybe. I don't know why, though. Must be something you said to him on the phone today."

"I guess."

The thick man was patting him down, feeling for concealed weapons in the too-large, ill-fitting jacket he had purchased hastily at a cheap haberdashery that afternoon.

"You hear the news?" Jersey asked conversationally as the other man searched.

"Oh, yeah. On TV. Showgirl commits suicide with gas oven. Clean job, Jersey, beautiful. So why didn't you just grab the noon flight and blow town? Why show your face out here tonight and bother Mr. R?"

Ricci entered the room. He was fully dressed, despite the lateness of the hour. He liked to look like a kingpin gang boss of the Thirties, and to that end he was always dressed as if costumed for a movie—in a custom-made, fitted, pinstripe suit, plus silk shirt, silk necktie, and shoes of Italian craftsmanship, made in Rome on a last shaped from his own foot. Only because he was at present indoors he was not wearing his famous broad-brimmed Borsalino hat and wraparound dark glasses. He had iron-gray hair and was about fifty years of age.

The thick man, finished patting down Jersey, said, "He's clean, Mr. Rich."

Jersey indelicately scratched his crotch.

The thick man laughed coarsely and said, "You got crabs, Jersey?"

"Just a little jock itch."

"Let's get this over with," Ricci said with distaste.

Jersey said, "I'm surprised at you, Sally. And a little disappointed. You tried to cheat me."

The thick man stepped forward. "Don't talk to Mr. Rich that way."

"Ease off, Mario," said Ricci.

"You tried to hire me for a lousy hundred," said Jersey, "when you know damn well that my price for Federal heat is half a mill."

Ricci smiled. "You found out, huh?"

"I found out. So you don't owe me just fifty grand. You owe me *four hundred* and fifty. And I'm here to collect it. In large bills, please."

Ricci turned to the thick man. "Get the money, Mario."

"Four-fifty??"

"Large bills, like the man said." When Mario was out of the room, Ricci said, "You're smart, Jersey. But it wasn't such a smart move coming here. Up to now, nobody knew what the famous Jersey looked like. You were just a couple of p.o. box numbers, a phone number, a recorded voice on an answering gadget, a man without a face. But now I've seen your face. So has Mario. Is that smart?"

"If it's dumb," said Jersey, "it's half a million clams' worth of dumb."

11

Ricci chuckled. "Probably the biggest score you ever chalked up, isn't it?"

"Petty cash to you, Sally."

"Hell, this puts you in the major leagues. International stuff. Political assassinations. Presidents . . . prime ministers. . . . Pretty soon you'll be doing just one or two a year and sitting on your keister the rest of the time. Might even be able to afford a decent suit of clothes!"

Mario returned with a briefcase that he placed before his boss. "Give it to our guest," said Ricci, and Mario reluctantly handed it over to Jersey.

He opened it and gave the money a quick count. Then he methodically began to stuff the brick-size stacks of bills into various inner and outer pockets of his deliberately loose jacket, saying, "I don't like briefcases." As he stuffed he said, "Just to make sure there are no more misunderstandings, this is four hundred and fifty thousand bucks, right?" Ricci nodded, bored. "Which," Jersey continued, still jamming money into his pockets until only a fraction was left in the case, "added to the fifty thousand you've already paid me, totals five hundred thousand dollars. And the total sum represents payment in full for snuffing the Kittering broad, right?"

"Payment in full, right," said Ricci. "No tips, gratuities, Christmas bonuses, or pension plans."

But Jersey wasn't smiling. "Thank you," he said. "Salvatore Ricci, Mario Fontana, you are both under arrest for conspiracy to murder a Federal investigator and making use of the United States Postal Service to bring it about, plus a whole lot of other trifles I won't annoy you with right now. . . ."

"What the hell is this?" snarled Ricci.

His visitor, offering I.D., replied, "What this is, is my calling card. It says that I'm Special Agent Dodd, Federal Bureau of Investigation. You have the right to remain silent—"

12

Instead of remaining silent, Ricci roared. "You rotten creep! You think you can put away Big Sally? Think this makes you king of the hill? Fair-haired boy of the FBI?"

"Oh, I hope so," said Special Agent Dodd with a wistful sigh. "I've been waiting for a big score like this for a long time. With what I've got on you, and what Investigator Kittering gathered on you, I figure you'll pull about two hundred years, give or take."

"I won't serve one day!"

"You may be right."

"Where's Jersey?" Ricci demanded.

"Still in Jersey," Special Agent Dodd assured him. "Six feet of it, in fact. He was gunned down by Federal agents last month. We managed to keep it quiet. And Mario?" he added suddenly, addressing the thick man. "If you go for that heater, the agents surrounding the house will rush in and buy you six feet of Nevada right now. There are a couple of dozen of them outside, and they're listening to every word, due to the fact that I'm wired. You didn't frisk me in the right places. Guess you didn't want to get too personal. They've also neutralized all those urban gorillas you had patrolling the premises. Just hand that cannon over to me, Mario. Thanks. Now, then, if I may continue, you gentlemen have the right to remain silent . . ."

There weren't a couple of dozen agents outside the Ricci house. There were only half a dozen. One of them, an anxious youth named Farnsworth, addressed Special Agent Dodd as he left the house with the briefcase. "You okay, Dodd? We thought we heard two shots in there."

"I'm fine. But Ricci and Fontana attempted to escape, so, unfortunately, I had to use deadly force." He shrugged. "Oh, well. Murder, extortion, narcotics, child prostitution . . . those two won't be missed, and it'll save the taxpayers a lot of money. A couple of bullets don't cost much."

"But you were unarmed . . ."

"I used Fontana's piece." Dodd handed the .45 Star PD automatic to the younger agent. "Here, you'd better take charge of it. Did you get everything on tape?"

"No. Almost nothing! Soon after you entered the house, everything went dead. We figure the wire attached to the crotch mike must have pulled loose."

"What a pity. Here, you'd better take charge of this, too." He handed over the briefcase. "And don't let it out of your sight. It contains fifty thousand cherrystones, and it'd better all be there when we turn it in with the other fifty thousand I picked up at the post office this morning."

Special Agent Farnsworth grinned. "Sure you don't want to boost a few dollars to buy yourself a better jacket? Looks like you got that one from the Nevada Tent and Awning Company."

"Very funny," said Special Agent Dodd.

14

3

T HE first thing he did after landing at Washington National Airport was to commandeer a cab and take it to the nearest bank, where he rented a safe deposit box.

The next day he visited Arthur Adler's, where he was measured for three exquisite suits of English cut, paying an additional charge for an early fitting date.

One of the suits was ready just in time for his lunch appointment with the Bureau Director later that week, at the Director's club. Dodd had never been invited to lunch by the Director before. It was a great honor.

The club's members were senators, governors, foreign diplomats, heads of state, deposed heads of state, former U.S. presidents, oil sheikhs, high-ranking corporation executives (domestic and Japanese), some Episcopal bishops, a Catholic cardinal, and one Supreme Court judge. The Bureau's only representative was the Director. There were no female members, despite the efforts and protests of feminist organizations. A small number of members, and all of the waiters, were black. The carpet was as thick as a lawn.

Rarely, but not rarely enough to suit the Director, a distinguished member would invite a gentleman from the Soviet Embassy to lunch at the club. "I can always spot them, even if they're wearing American suits," he had claimed. "They all have rectangular faces, like shoe boxes."

The Director, a man in his late fifties, was somewhat rectangular himself, and looked as if he had just stepped out of a barber's chair, after a light trim, creamy shave, five or six lotions, and scalding towels. But, Dodd reflected, he always looked like that, any hour of the day or night. Yank him out of bed at two in the morning and he'd probably look like that.

They drank gibsons the size of hubcaps and ate lobster in port cream. With the lobster, they drank a crisp Pouilly-Fuissé.

"How did you like Las Vegas?" the Director asked.

"Not very much, sir. The climate's too dry for my taste. I began to feel like an emery board."

The Director smiled. "Some people find Washington too humid. In the old days it was considered a tropical hardship post by some of the European countries, and they paid their diplomats bonuses to serve here."

"I didn't know that."

"It's in the history books." The Director chewed his lobster thoughtfully. "How is it, Dodd," he asked, "that you haven't come to my attention before this?"

"Well, I keep a low profile, sir."

"We all do, naturally. None of us is Robert Stack or Kevin Costner, eh?"

"No, sir." Dodd grinned politely.

"But, although I discourage flamboyance, I must say I find very little to criticize in your handling of the recent Las Vegas situation."

"Thank you, sir."

"More wine?"

"Just a drop, maybe."

"Not too dry for your taste, like Las Vegas?"

"No, sir. Just right."

The Director poured, saying, "You came near to losing your life, I understand."

Dodd shrugged. "It was a bit touch-and-go."

"You went into that house unarmed?"

"Had to, sir. I knew they'd pat me down, and they did."

The Director's eyes widened with amazement. "And then you simply identified yourself and told those desperadoes that they were under arrest?"

Desperadoes. Dodd hadn't heard that word in years.

"More or less. Yes, sir. That's when Fontana pulled the gun on me and I disarmed him. Then both of them tried to jump me, and—I had to fire. Thought I could just wound them, but at those close quarters . . . well, you know what they say, it's a dirty job, but—"

"Nobody's blaming you," said the Director. "Oh, some of the media knee-jerks may get a little hot under the collar after we decide to release the news. The ACLU may make a little noise. But that needn't bother you. They don't speak for the American people." The Director smiled and shook his head with admiration. "Just two rounds fired, and a pair of vicious rattlesnakes get it right between the eyes. You don't waste any ammunition, do you, son?"

"Well, sir," replied Dodd, "I figure the taxpayer has a big enough burden already." He sipped the Pouilly-Fuissé and forked up another bite of lobster.

"Where did you learn to shoot like that? The NYPD?"

"That's right, sir."

"Well, I think a promotion has been overdue, Dodd. But now I'm expecting even bigger and better things from you." Dodd wasn't at all sure what he meant by that. "Of course," the Director added hastily, "I realize that you didn't work alone. This lad Farnsworth must have been a great help to you, for instance. . . ."

Yes, Dodd wanted to say, when he wasn't stepping on his own shoelaces. "Special Agent Farnsworth's a good man, sir. And, to give credit where credit is due, Field

Investigator Kittering's contribution to the operation was incalculable."

"Kittering. . . . Ah, yes, the Justice Department girl. . . ."

"You know, sir," said Dodd, "if you don't mind my saying it, there's sometimes a little too much rivalry between the Bureau and the Justice Department."

The Director chuckled tolerantly. "A bit of competition is a healthy thing, Dodd. Keeps all of us on our toes."

"Absolutely, sir. I agree. I just mean that sometimes operations might mesh better if the Bureau and Justice took the chips off their shoulders and occasionally did things together."

"No doubt, no doubt," muttered the Director. "Are you ready for dessert and coffee?"

Dodd was. And when lunch with the Director was over, he was ready for other things. Dodd was no longer feeling like a convalescent but like a new man. It may have been the lunch, he told himself as he stifled a belch, it may have been the new suit, it may have been the hint of promotion, it may have been his recent big score in Vegas, it may have been a combination of all the above.

But more likely, he mentally added, it was the eager anticipation of the second lunch engagement he was now on his way to keeping—this one with Field Investigator Kittering.

The late lunch took place at her apartment. In view of the fact that Dodd had just gorged, he sipped Scotch, watched her nibble at a dieter's lettuce-and-grapefruit snack, and shook his head in disapproval.

"What's wrong?" she asked.

"I can't believe you're eating that."

"Why not? It's low calorie, rich in vitamins, minerals, fiber, very good for you, all natural."

"Natural. Listen. Nature is great. To look at. Trees, mountains. But not to *eat*. Not *raw*. That's why cooking was invented. That stuff will kill you. It goes through your body like razor blades."

"Thanks for the nutrition lesson. I've got frozen tofu dessert in the fridge, want some?"

"Actually, I had another kind of dessert in mind." He waggled his eyebrows roguishly.

"Actually, so did I."

After dessert, they talked.

"How was your lunch with the Director?" she asked.

"Two thousand calories, easy. He patted me on the head and made noises about a possible promotion."

"Chief?"

"Good Lord, no. Probably Supervisory Special Agent. There's a nice raise goes with that."

"Is that what you meant, in Vegas, when you said that if you scored big, you could get into a branch of your business that was safer and paid more money?"

"I guess so. Of course, I didn't know who you were then, so I had to pussyfoot. Incidentally, I put in a good word for you, too."

"Thanks for nothing. Your Director isn't my boss."

"I know, I know. I just wanted you to know that I give you credit. And I'm always thinking about you."

She smiled and kissed him. "You've got a heart as big as all indoors."

After several moments he said hoarsely, "I should be getting back to the salt mines."

"What, *you?* The fair-haired boy? Who'd *dare* criticize you for taking a long lunch, particularly when you were out with the Director?"

"Hell, it's almost three o'clock. Some lunch! And what about you? Don't you have to get back?"

"I took a couple of extra hours for a doctor's appointment."

He grinned. "Very therapeutic for both the patient and the doctor," he assured her, just as her telephone rang.

"Excuse me," she said, reaching out a creamy arm from her bed to lift the phone. "Hello? . . . Yes, sir. . . . I see. . . . Oh, that's wonderful. . . . I'm so glad. . . . Thanks for calling, sir. . . . Good-bye." She hung up.

"Good news?" he inquired.

"Very good. They just opened your safe deposit box. Hey, are you all right?"

He had gone as white and clammy as a peeled egg.

She said, "Your protegé, Farnsworth, got suspicious of your baggy jacket and tailed you to the bank when you rented the box. He came to me for assistance in getting authority to open it because he was afraid you might have too much clout at the Bureau. I created enough red tape to delay things until I was able to bull my way solo into the box by just waving my credentials, not to mention my ass, at the bank manager. I removed what I found there and substituted a Gideon Bible. That's what *they* found when they opened the box ten minutes ago. No crime in keeping a Bible in a bank vault. I figured we'd split the money seventy-five–twenty-five, in my favor."

He shook his head. "Fifty-fifty."

"Deal."

She swung her long legs out of bed and walked across the bedroom, barefoot up to the eyebrows, as the saying goes, giving Dodd a lingering view of the elongated-8 shape of her back and her world-class buttocks. "Tell me something, Dodd," she said, pouring herself a glass of water from a carafe on the dressing table.

"Sure. What?"

She drank the water, and walked back to the bed, giving him another lingering view, this time of her groan-invoking front: geometrically rounded breasts, faintly convex abdomen, private hair that was a fiery perfect match for the blaze of her head; and all that dizzying expanse of pelt so smooth, smooth, smooth, of a smoothness to make the slickest satin rough as a cat's tongue.

"At what point did you decide to rip off the money?" she asked as she climbed back into bed. "Right from the start?"

"Of course not. Only after I found out you were Federal fuzz. That's when I knew I could get more out of Big Sally, and nobody else would know about it if I could silence those two maggots and disconnect the crotch wire. And I wasn't sure I *had* disconnected the wire until I checked with Farnsworth, so I didn't hand over the short-changed money in the briefcase until he told me he had nothing on tape. Hell, if I had planned it from the start, would I have waited till the last minute to buy that dumb jacket?"

"Poor Farnsie," she said.

"He'll get over it." The color had returned to his face. "It's like I told the Director at lunch today," he said. "Things would go smoother if the Bureau and the Justice Department stopped fighting each other and did things *together.*"

"I agree," she said, suiting action to word. "But you know, technically, your Bureau is just one of the divisions of the Justice Department, and actually is supposed to work . . . um . . . *under* the Department. Figuratively speaking."

"Very funny," said Special Agent Dodd.

4

"YOU wanted to see me, Chief?"
Supervisory Special Agent Dodd said this as he entered the office of his superior the following week.

The office was large, deep-carpeted, many-windowed. Covering an entire wall was an immense map of the United States. An American flag stood in one corner. A large globe of the world occupied another corner—almost as if the Chief yearned to stretch his influence beyond the borders of his country. Several reproductions of oil portraits hung on the walls: George Washington, Abraham Lincoln, J. Edgar Hoover, the current President of the United States, and the current Director of the Federal Bureau of Investigation.

A longstanding enigma was the cluster of smaller portraits that stared cryptically from another wall. Only a few of them had been immediately recognizable to Dodd the first time he had seen them, and they were a strange sextet, indeed: the notorious murderers Loeb and Leopold, plus Lenin, Woodrow Wilson, Rocky Marciano, and Marlene Dietrich. Some of the others he had identified, one by one, over the months and years, more or less by accident. An old-time actress, Eleanora Duse. A few composers, among them George Gershwin, Victor Herbert, Giacomo Puccini. Doug Fairbanks, Senior, in a scene from some old movie. Louella Parsons, a gossip columnist of the past. A lot of writers: Faulkner, Capote, Melville, Mann, Kafka, Conrad, even Wodehouse. There was an idealized watercolor of the quintessential American Indian. And, far more normal for an FBI wall, there was a "Wanted" poster of a glaring gray-haired man identified as D. D. ("Bearcat") Stutz, a.k.a. King of the Big Time Gamblers. But the rest of the faces in the gallery Dodd had never been able to nail. And he would die before he'd ask the Chief who they were or what they were doing on his wall.

The Chief was sitting behind a desk that was clean and bare and shining enough to perform surgery upon. His chair was swiveled around so that his back was to Dodd. He was facing the windows, looking out across the street—Pennsylvania Avenue—at the Department of Justice building opposite. The chair wheeled slowly back into its normal position and the Chief fixed his gaze upon Dodd. His eyes were the color of a wet sidewalk.

"Working here in this nice new J. Edgar Hoover Building as we do," he said, "we enjoy an advantage over all other Washingtonians. Do you know what that is, Dodd?"

"No, Chief."

"We don't have to *look* at this nice new J. Edgar Hoover Building. It's not only the ugliest structure in the Federal Triangle. It has got to be the single most atrociously hideous piece of architecture in the entire District. I will include the state of Maryland and the Commonwealth of Virginia."

"Yes, Chief."

The Chief sighed. "Are you a religious man?"

Dodd replied, "Chief, I thought the religious preferences of agents were considered to be their own concern, and of no interest to the Bureau."

"I didn't ask about your religious *preferences*, Dodd. I asked, simply, are you religious?"

Shrugging, Dodd said, "I guess I'm as religious as the next man, Chief."

"In my experience," snapped the Chief, "the 'next man' has about as much use for religion as he has for an extra sleeve. So why do you keep a Bible in a safe deposit box?"

"I've been meaning to ask you about that, Chief."

"*You've* been meaning to ask *me*?"

"Yes," said Dodd. "I was just wondering if the Bureau would like to inspect any of my other private possessions. My apartment? My locker at the gym? Trunk of my car? Just let me know, sir, and I'll hand over the keys."

"That's quite all right, Dodd," said the Chief with a heart-stopping smile. "Those places have already been inspected. I was surprised to learn that you stock frozen tofu dessert in your freezer. Somehow it just doesn't seem you."

"I keep it for a friend. Am I off the hook, then, Chief?"

"About the tofu? Yes."

"I mean, am I no longer under suspicion?"

"Suspicion of what?"

"You tell me, Chief."

"Do you feel we've violated your Constitutional rights, Dodd?"

"Nope."

"Not going to sic the ACLU on us?"

"Wouldn't dream of it."

"Good. Now maybe you'll be so kind as to answer my question."

"What question was that, Chief?"

"Why do you keep a Bible in a safe deposit box?"

"Sentimental reasons."

"What?"

"My mother gave it to me."

"Your mother!? Aren't you forgetting it's a *Gideon* Bible? Purloined from a hotel room? With *Powers Hotel, Fargo, North Dakota* rubber-stamped all over it?"

"That's where my parents spent their honeymoon. I was conceived in that hotel room. Sentimental, as I said."

The Chief growled. "It has been suggested that the Bible is part of a book code."

"Book code?"

"That's right, Dodd. You know what a book code is, don't you? Both parties have identical editions of the same book, any book. To transmit secret messages, all they have to do is indicate page, line, and number for every word in the message. If you have the book, you can figure it out easily, but if you don't, it's just a lot of gibberish."

"Oh, *that* kind of book code."

"Yes, that kind."

"More likely to be in the CIA's line than ours, don't you think, Chief? International espionage and all?"

"In the normal course of events," the Chief conceded. "If there aren't any aberrations."

"Aberrations?"

"That's the word the Bureau uses when its agents are caught slipping secrets to Soviet spies."

"You think that's what I've been doing, Chief?"

"I don't know what you've been doing, Dodd. Why don't you tell me?"

"Okay, I will. My job. That's what I've been doing. Like putting the Ricci mob out of business . . ."

"And into the cemetery, while you were at it, planted next to that New Jersey hit man you canceled last month. The name of Dodd is becoming a ghoulish joke around the Bureau. They say 'As Dodd is my judge.' Get it? As if you were God? Is that the way you see yourself? God?"

"We've already established that I'm not very religious," Dodd reminded him. "I just do my job. And lately I've been doing it good enough to earn a promotion and private lunch meetings with the Director. I'll tell you what I *haven't* been doing. I haven't been playing footsie with the Russians or any other foreign spies. And I haven't been using that book for any kind of code. I'll swear to it."

The Chief leered. "On a stack of Bibles?"

Dodd returned the leer. "Better than that. On a polygraph."

"You *will*?"

"I will."

"You'll allow yourself to be hooked up to a lie detector while you're asked questions about your mother's Bible and—"

Dodd cut in: "I will swear that I am not working for the Russians or any other foreign power, and I will swear that I am not using any kind of code, book code or otherwise, involving that Bible or any other Bible or any other book of any kind, but I will *not* permit any reference to my mother to be bandied about in any polygraph test. If the *word* 'mother' so much as crosses the lips of the polygraph operator, that operator will end up in traction for six months. Sir."

The Chief grew red, then white, then gray as gunpowder.

"That will be all, Dodd."

"Yes, Chief."

Dodd turned and walked to the door. As his hand touched the knob, he turned back and asked, "When shall we schedule the polygraph test for, Chief?"

The voice of Jenny Lind, the fabled Swedish Nightingale, could not have sounded sweeter than that of the Chief when he said, "I think we'll scrub the test. After all, the polygraph is only a machine, made by mortal men. And you, Dodd, are the son of the Father of Lies himself. One of these days you're going to lie yourself straight into Hell."

"Thanks, Chief. Takes one to know one."

Dodd left the office, and the Bureau building, and the Federal Triangle, on his way to an early and solitary lunch. Before eating, he found a lonely outdoor pay phone and, giving his charge card a rest so there would be no record of the call on his account, he fed enough coins into the phone to make a connection to New York City.

"Hello?" a woman's voice answered.

"Hi, Ma," said Dodd.

"Kiddo? That you?"

"Who else calls you Ma?"

"That's right! You were my only accident!" She cackled merrily. "How are you, honey?"

"Never better. I got a promotion, a raise, and a new girlfriend. How are *you*?"

"Not bad for an old broad. But I'm between boy-friends."

"What happened to Hugo?"

"*Otto*, not Hugo. I threw him out. Long story. Boring."

"That's okay. I like boring stories."

"No, I mean Otto was boring. Never mind. That's great news about the promotion and everything. Thanks for the birthday card."

"You're welcome. Listen, Ma, I've forgotten, if I ever knew—where did you spend your honeymoon?"

"Which one?"

"My dad."

"Oh, Number Two. Dodd. Gee, that was a long time ago. Let me see. Oh, yeah, of course. Hawaii."

"Uh-huh."

"Had a great time there. Then we settled down in his hometown, Chicago, where he had a very nice job, and we got ourselves an apartment on what they used to call the Near North Side. Maybe they still call it that. Near to *what*, I never knew. We were yuppies."

"Ma, they didn't have yuppies back in the Fifties."

"They didn't call them that, but we were yuppies, all right. Your father and I, and all our friends, we went to all the yuppie foreign movies—*Rashomon, Kind Hearts and Coronets*—and we all had wall masks and folk music records and tall green glass bottles standing next to the fireplaces in our apartments. Some of us even smoked pot. No cocaine, though. Do you remember tall green glass bottles?"

"Too young," said Dodd. "But I remember the wall masks. They used to scare the hell out of me. Did you have lava lamps, too?"

"Lava lamps were later. The Sixties."

"Ah. Right. Now listen, Ma. I want you to pay close attention. This is very important. It's a *Bureau operation*, understand?"

"I'm hip."

"Fine. Someone may ask you where you spent your honeymoon with Mr. Dodd. That someone may be *anybody*. The butcher, the baker, the candlestick maker. Your closest friend, maybe. They may even tell you they're from the Bureau. They may even show you some very authentic-looking credentials. But, Ma, don't tell them Hawaii."

"Okay, I won't. Why not?"

"Because you'll *blow my cover*."

"Gotcha. Bureau business. Top secret."

"Right."

"So what do I say?"

"You say Fargo, North Dakota."

"What??"

"The Powers Hotel in Fargo, North Dakota."

"What a dumb place to spend a honeymoon."

"Can you remember that?"

"Of course I can. You think I'm senile? For the love of Pete, I'm only sixty! Powers Hotel, Fargo, South Dakota."

"North Dakota!"

"North, South . . . okay, I got it."

"Love ya, Ma, Gotta go."

"Kiddo?"

"Yes?"

"Is she pretty, the new girlfriend?"

"Gorgeous."

"Good for you."

"Bye, Ma. It's always a slice of life talking to you."

After he hung up, he spotted a man across the street, hiding behind the *National Enquirer*. Dodd jaywalked directly up to him and said, "You'll rot your brain reading that stuff."

Special Agent Farnsworth lowered the paper and responded, "What do you suggest? The Bible?"

"You could do worse. What are you doing out here, Farnsie? They got you pounding a beat? Well, at least you're in the fresh air. I was afraid they'd have you separating paper clips. Come on, I'll buy you lunch. You look like you're suffering from a serious case of cholesterol deficiency."

"No, thanks," Farnsworth said sourly. "I'm on special assignment."

"Okay," said Dodd, "but if you change your mind, I'll be putting away shrimp cocktail and prime rib at Chaucer's."

"Living high on the hog, aren't you, Dodd? Lunch at Chaucer's, new suits. Whatever became of that circus tent you were wearing in Vegas?"

"I thought I might give it away to some deserving clown. You want it?"

"Spending a lot of money, aren't you?"

"Well," said Dodd, "I got a raise, you know."

"I thought maybe someone died and left you a bundle."

"I don't have any rich relatives, Farnsie," said Dodd. He placed one hand over his heart and held the other up in a nothing-but-the-truth gesture, adding, "As Dodd is my judge."

5

ACTUALLY, Dodd didn't lunch at the Chaucer restaurant in the Canterbury Hotel—he'd said that just to throw Farnsworth off the track. He lunched at the Jockey Club, where he sampled their famous double-digit crab cakes. He would have liked to have lunched with Kittering, but they had agreed it was wiser not to be seen together socially, at least not for a while.

After lunch, he placed a call to her at Justice, but was told she wasn't in. Two hours later he called again and got the same response.

That evening he called her apartment twice but received no answer. He wanted to see her very much. His flesh yearned for her, that glowing body, but it was more than that: he smiled at the way her mind worked, the way she talked.

He also wanted to find out where she had stashed the money.

But tomorrow was another day. He climbed into bed and was soon asleep.

He dreamed he was lying in bed—that very bed—and his father was sitting in the chair at his side.

"Hi, Dad."

"How you doing, kid?"

"Pretty good, in fact. What are *you* doing here?"

"Well, don't get all shook up or anything, but they sent me here to come and get you. Your number came up is the cornball way they put it. I told them you're too young, but go fight city hall. Actually, I can give you a few days to put your affairs in order. You know, last will and testament or whatever. Then you and me, we'll go off together. Don't bother to pack. You know what they say, you can't take it with you."

Dodd asked, "Do they always send fathers?"

"Usually it's the mother. But your mother is still alive. If both parents are still alive, they send a grandparent."

"How . . . how will it happen, Dad?"

"Hey, I don't know. Really, kid, they wouldn't tell me. If I knew, I'd tell you. But I suppose they know what they're doing. You *are* in a dangerous business, though." He chuckled. "Hey, that was some fast one you pulled with that money, huh?"

"You know about that?"

"Oh, yeah. We know everything."

"Dad?"

"Yeah?"

"What's it like . . . where you are?"

"Not bad. Hard to describe. You ever been to Nova Scotia? A little bit like that. But they say it gets better."

Urgently Dodd said, "Dad, there's something I've always wanted to know. After—"

The telephone yanked him out of sleep suddenly and cruelly. He pawed at it in the dark and spoke thickly into the wrong end: "Hullo?"

"Dodd? That you? Something wrong with this connection?"

No mistaking that voice. Dodd righted the phone, snapped on the bedside light, and squinted at the clock. It was a shade past two-thirty.

"Dodd speaking. What's up, Chief?"

"*I'm* up, and I want *you* up and in my office *on the double*. Don't even comb your hair." Crash. Dial tone.

He was blinking at the Chief well before three o'clock.

31

"Sit down, Dodd. We've got a problem."

Dodd sat and waited, silent. Had they found out about the money? Was that why he hadn't been able to get in touch with Kittering? He began to worry.

"As you know," said the Chief, "a number of arrests were recently made in Las Vegas, thanks to you and Farnsworth and other Bureau agents, working with an investigator from Justice, and hand in hand with the Drug Enforcement Administration and other agencies."

Dodd nodded. It didn't look good.

"I'm sure you're also aware," the Chief went on, "that the arrested individuals are facing indictment on several counts under the RICO act."

Dodd nodded again, although, if truth were told, he would have been forced to admit that he wasn't quite awake enough to remember that the Chief was referring to the Racketeer Influenced and Corrupt Organizations act of 1970, a useful piece of legislation that, in addition to bringing about a number of successful Mafia prosecutions, also had been used against international drug traffickers, foreign coup organizers, terrorists, and even certain white-collar frauds.

At that moment Dodd would have agreed to strangle his Chief in return for a cup of coffee and a French doughnut.

"But not everybody is happy about those impending indictments," said the Chief.

Certainly not the arrested individuals, Dodd almost said but didn't.

"The Justice Department has received a demand for the release of one of the prisoners," said the Chief.

"Demand? Who from?"

The Chief slid out from behind his desk and walked over to the globe of the world that occupied a corner of his office. Dodd followed him. The Chief twirled the sphere until the huge landmasses of the Americas came into view. His finger stabbed the bright blue water off the southernmost tip of South America as he said, "Down here just off the Horn, in the water near the place where Chile and Argentina dovetail and jigsaw together: do you see all these little islands, this scattering of birdseed?"

"Just barely."

"Some of the bigger ones have names. Look at this— Wellington, Hanover, Londonderry! There'll always be an England, eh? And I love this one—Desolación. But the spot we're looking for isn't even on my globe here, isn't on most maps. It's around *here* someplace, a flyspeck called La Calavera."

"Pretty name," said Dodd.

The Chief returned to his desk, Dodd following. "La Calavera is just far enough off the coast to be out of the jurisdiction of either Chile or Argentina. The head honcho there, El Presidente, is a former Chilean named Ysidro Vásquez Gutiérrez."

One of the Chief's phones rang. He scooped it up, saying, "Yes? . . . A positive match, you're sure? Thanks." Slamming it down, he said, "Where was I?"

"This Gutiérrez. Do we have a file on him?"

"Thick as a mattress," said the Chief. "So does the CIA. So does the DEA. So does the KGB. And his surname is Vásquez, incidentally, even though it's in the middle. That's the Hispanic way. He's a law unto himself, and probably the most powerful *coquero* in the world."

"Does that mean what it sounds like?"

"I'm afraid it does. It means he's a king of cocaine, and he runs what the DEA assures me is the biggest single coke network on this planet. Or any other planet, let's hope. He's also branched into epadu."

"Come again?"

"A hardy shrub that doesn't need the mountain slopes of Bolivia or Peru to grow on, like the coca plant does. It can do very nicely, thank you, in forests and jungles— which Brazil, say, mostly is. Epadu yields the same active ingredient as coca—some kind of alkaloid, I'm told—and it's easier to grow. Vásquez owns 'illegal' epadu plantations—" The Chief scratched the air with two fingers of each hand to indicate a mockery of illegality. "—in Brazil, coca plantations in Bolivia, Peru, and now Ecuador, and refineries in all those places plus Panama, Venezuela, Argentina, and—through the late Mr. Ricci—Miami."

Dodd whistled. "But nothing in his own, his native land?"

"La Calavera has the wrong climate for growing. Besides, he wants to keep the place respectable. That's where he lives."

"Actually, I meant Chile."

"Are you serious? Not while the present regime calls the shots there. Shots *literally*, as in brick wall. *Coqueros* are *really* illegal in Chile, which is why Vásquez was condemned to the firing squad there a few years ago. A corrupt cop helped him escape, but if he ever sets foot inside Chile again, he's a dead man. He's a billionaire now, in his mid-forties, wears a patch over the hole in his face where a Chilean police chief personally thumbed out his right eye, considers himself a devoté of the opera, and—to give you the complete picture—was educated at, or flung out of, Oxford, the Sorbonne, Harvard, and UCLA. Oh, a very cultivated gentleman, is President Vásquez. Here: this is what he looks like, as of eight months ago, which is as recent as our information gets."

Dodd found himself looking at the front page of a Spanish-language newspaper called *Verdad*, featuring the handsome, eye-patched face of Vásquez. "That's the official, and only, newspaper of La Calavera," said the Chief. "*Verdad* means Truth, like *Pravda* means Truth. Vásquez owns the paper. Anyway, he's demanding the release of one of his Las Vegas associates and the safe conveyance of said associate to La Calavera."

"Why?" asked Dodd.

34

"The man he wants released is a VIP, it seems—his U.S. representative in the cocaine trade."

Dodd frowned. "But the only collars we made in Vegas were those three-piece crocodiles guarding Ricci's house. Hard to believe that any of those muscleheads could be the U.S. rep for a drug operation that big."

The Chief smiled monstrously. "How true," he said. "The man Vásquez wants is Salvatore Ricci."

Dodd's eyes snapped wide open for the first time that morning. *"But he's—"*

"Is he?" inquired the Chief, still smiling. "Not officially. We've only leaked news of some 'major Mafia arrests' in Las Vegas. Vásquez undoubtedly got wind of that, tried to contact Ricci, came up empty, and assumed we've got him in durance vile."

Dodd shrugged. "So what's the problem, Chief?"

"The problem is that Vásquez had the foresight to take a hostage, whom he is now entertaining at La Calavera and whom he will proceed to dismantle, piece by piece, if we don't produce Big Sally."

"Then why don't we just tell him Big Sally's dead?"

"We did," said the Chief. "He didn't believe us."

"But he *is* dead!"

The Chief sighed. "That's not the point. The whole point is what we can make Vásquez *believe*. Put yourself in his shoes. If you were Vásquez, would *you* have believed us when we told you Ricci was dead?"

Dodd shook his head.

"It has been suggested," said the Chief, "that the only chance we have is to tell Vásquez we're complying with his demand."

"And *then* what?"

"And then, rather than send him Mr. Ricci—which of course we cannot do—we send him someone who can make him believe that Ricci is dead."

Shedding propriety, Dodd roared, "What idiot suggested *that?*"

"Our Director, may his tribe increase," said the Chief, extending a reverential hand toward the wall portrait of that personage. "He also suggested that *you* might be just the man for the job." With an acetylene sigh the Chief added, "He thinks the world of you."

"But Jesus Christ—"

"Name dropping will get you nowhere," purred the Chief. "I admit it may not be a brilliant idea, but do you have a better one? I pause for a reply. No, you do *not* have a better one. Remember, you'll have your famous ingenuity to fall back on, and your vaunted charisma, your gift of gab, all those qualities that have given the Director so much faith in you."

"The Bureau has no jurisdiction outside the U.S.," Dodd pointed out.

"That's why you'd have to resign from the Bureau and go down there unofficially, as a civilian. You'd be reinstated at your current rank and with no loss in pay or benefits upon your return. *If* you return. I think you stand a better than fifty-fifty chance of getting out alive."

"I think they'd shoot me the minute I stepped off the plane," Dodd said sourly. "You'd be sending me to certain death."

"I'm not sending you anywhere," the Chief said softly. "It's not the kind of thing I can order a man to do. But I hope you will. Because the hostage Vásquez is holding down there is one of our own—a member of law enforcement personnel—and we know that's true because we just got a positive match on the tip of the hostage's left little finger that we received early this morning."

"Anybody I know?"

"Field Investigator Kittering."

"Oh, shit," said Dodd.

He thought of her warmth, her wit, her beauty, and her bravery. To his credit, it was at least ten seconds before he thought about the money.

Part

6

To watch Ysidro Vásquez Gutiérrez, the President of La Calavera, crack a boiled egg was like watching a master diamond cutter at work on a stone of great price. With his left hand, he steadied the egg cup. With his right hand, he delicately balanced the butter knife, intuitively judging the proper force, the exact spot where the blow should fall. For a split second all was frozen as in a photograph, then—*tap!*— the crown of the egg fell to the plate, neatly decapitated. Vásquez put down the knife, reached for spoon and salt shaker, and began to eat his breakfast.

El Presidente and Señora Vásquez, his bride of six months, partook of that meal in an enclosed patio of the presidential palace. Outside rain clouds were gathering, typical of this climate. He was a swarthy Latin in early middle age, with hair still like black vinyl, despite his years. He no longer affected the eyepatch Dodd's Chief had mentioned, but in its place now sported a chocolate-brown glass eye that was an almost identical duplicate of its living counterpart.

The First Lady was an olive-skinned beauty with eyes as brown as her husband's and a mass of hair, thanks to the miracles of modern chemistry, that was as acidly yellow as lemons. Her décolletage could cleave the brain of any normal man between the ages of nine and ninety and cause him to foam from several body openings simultaneously. She was in the burstingly ripe peak of her mid-thirties, and therefore about a decade younger than Vásquez. She forked scrambled eggs into her bright-red mouth and said, "I *told* you she was lying."

"I always thought so," he agreed, lifting a napkin-swathed bottle of sparkling potation from an ice bucket and topping his goblet. "But when she persisted in keeping to her story even after her fingertip had been removed, I must admit I began to believe her."

"You used an *anesthetic!*" his wife said contemptuously. "Your personal *surgeon!* The palace *clinic!* She didn't feel a *thing!*" She snorted. "*I* would have gotten the truth out of her! I would have snipped off her jelly beans, cold turkey, *no* anesthetic! Rotten cop!"

As a servant cleared away their plates and another served the porridge, Vásquez said, "The object, *mi rosa*, was to obtain a souvenir for the Department of Justice. Something to identify the hostage and effectively illustrate the firmness of our position."

"Glad something's firm around here," muttered the lady.

"And it worked. Our dear Salvatore will be arriving—" He glanced at his wristwatch. "—in one hour, at La Calavera International Airport."

Señora Vásquez laughed raucously. "International Airport! That scrawny landing strip with one windsock and a Pepsi machine? Don't make me laugh, Izzy!"

"Please," he said, "not Izzy. Call me Ysidro, I beg of you, or at least the English equivalent, Isidore. Incidentally, I have invited Miss Kittering to join us for coffee."

"I'm not all that crazy about having coffee with the fuzz," grumbled Señora Vásquez.

"She is only a girl," said El Presidente. "And we are, after all, heads of state, engaged in an international negotiation. It behooves us to be civilized. Ah, here is the poached salmon." He lifted the napkined bottle from the ice bucket again. "Will you take a glass of Dr. Pepper with it, my love?"

"I'll stick with the coffee, thanks."

He shrugged and, gallantly touching his goblet to her cup with a clink, said, *"Mucho gusto!"*

The pilot of the aircraft began to see it now, even from this distance: the grim death's head that was his landmark. Hewn into the precipitous cliffside by cyclonic winds, in the form of caves, ridges, and other natural features, the island presented to all who approached it from this direction the forbidding face that gave the place its name: La Calavera.

The Skull.

He hated it. And he hated the dangerously short landing strip that began at the very edge of the cliff and did not extend far enough for reasonable safety. If a pilot overshot too far before touching down, he could run out of strip before he could bring his aircraft to a stop. If he came in even a fraction of an inch too low, he would collide with the mocking grin of the cliff.

It had happened in the past, more than once. Today, perhaps, it would happen again. With a quick, furtive gesture of his right hand, the pilot crossed himself.

He turned around and addressed his three passengers. The one they had picked up in Argentina was still wearing his hat and still holding on to that box. "Landing in twenty minutes, señores. Fasten your seat belts, please."

Field Investigator Kittering was conducted into the enclosed breakfast patio of El Presidente and Señora Vásquez.

"Ah," said Vásquez, rising. "So good of you to grace our table. My dear, Miss Kittering. Miss Kittering, Señora Vásquez, First Lady of La Calavera."

"Grab a seat," said the First Lady.

"What kind of coffee do you prefer?" asked El Presidente. "Colombian? Turkish? Espresso? Capuccino? *Café au lait* in the French manner?"

"Just plain coffee will be fine," said Kittering, "with a little milk."

"Colombian, then." Vásquez nodded to the hovering servant, who poured. "Sugar, Miss Kittering?"

"No, thank you."

After her first sip, he asked her, somewhat delicately, "You are experiencing . . . no great discomfort?"

She held up the bandaged little finger of her left hand. "Not really. It smarts a little once in a while."

"Once again I express my regret at your sacrifice," said Vásquez. "But it has proved to be gratifyingly effective. Your Justice Department has agreed to put Mr. Ricci on board a plane, and he is expected here as soon as you finish your coffee."

Kittering put down her cup suddenly. "He *is?*"

"Yeah," said Señora Vásquez. "What do you say to *that?*"

"I don't know what to say."

"I bet you don't. All that stuff about him being dead!"

"I was told that he was," said Kittering.

"And I believe that *you* believed it," El Presidente said chivalrously. "But in a matter of minutes we will all go to La Calavera International Airport to await his arrival and to welcome him. It will be a gala occasion. The Calavera Symphony Orchestra, under the baton of Maestro Ottokar Schütz, will be there to accompany the great basso Luigi Albericho, whom I have engaged. In honor of Mr. Ricci's native city, Palermo, he will sing the beautiful aria, 'O tu, Palermo,' from Verdi's opera *I Vespri Siciliani, The Sicilian Vespers*. The entire opera will be performed here next week by the Calavera Opera Company at the Calavera Open Air Grand Opera Theatre and Soccer Court. They are even now in rehearsal for the great event. Of course, the company has been imported from Europe, at enormous expense."

"And the soda pop has been imported from the States," cracked the Señora. "Want a little shot of Dr. Pepper in your coffee, honey?"

"No, thanks."

"It pleases my lady wife to jest," said Vásquez, "but indeed I fancy myself a connoisseur of your American soft drinks. I have a well-stocked cellar of them, under carefully monitored refrigeration." He glanced at his watch. "Come, ladies. If you have finished your coffee, it is time we were wending our way to the airport. The limousine awaits."

A liveried chauffeur drove the long, hearselike limo to La Calavera International Airport, what there was of it. The journey took all of twelve minutes. La Calavera was a small island. Small, cold, barren, windswept, and wet. At the moment, however, it was not raining. "Thanks for small mercies," growled Señora Vásquez.

As the limousine slowed to a stop, a massive man in military uniform walked up to it, saluting. His mustaches were like the horns of an ox, and his eyebrows resembled black fur awnings. "Señor Presidente!" he said in clipped tones as Vásquez stepped out. "Señora!" he added, ogling the First Lady's cleavage as she bent to leave the car.

"I see that you have marshalled your troops, General Espinoza," said Vásquez, addressing the officer in Spanish.

"Only a small detachment, Presidente."

Vásquez shrugged. "To meet our own plane, carrying my esteemed associate? Hardly necessary. . . ."

"Perhaps not, Presidente, but I have adopted the motto of the United States Marine Corps: 'Be prepared.'"

"Admirable," said Vásquez, "although I believe that is the motto of the Boy Scouts of America. No matter. Ah, I see the musicians are here. Have the goodness, General,

43

to pay your respects to the Señora and Miss Kittering while I speak to the artists."

Maestro Ottokar Schütz, Signor Luigi Albericho, and the Calavera Symphony Orchestra had already assembled, shivering, in the damp grasses just off the landing strip. The members of the orchestra were seated on folding chairs; Albericho paced nervously in the grass as if he were backstage at the opera house; Schütz stood calmly surveying the orchestra through narrowed eyes, hands behind his back, baton tucked under his armpit.

Vásquez, excusing himself to the two ladies, walked over to Schütz and beckoned to Albericho. "As we discussed, gentlemen, the selection will begin when we see Mr. Ricci emerge from the aircraft, not before."

"How vill ve know him?" asked Schütz.

"I will know him," said Vásquez, "and I will give you the signal. Remember: we will dispense with the recitative and go directly to the aria." Both men nodded. Vásquez returned to General Espinoza and the women.

"This whole opera thing was a dumb idea," said Señora Vásquez. "Salvatore hates opera as much as I do."

"Even if that is true," said her husband, "he cannot fail to respond to a song about his native city, sung in the language of his childhood by a fine Sicilian artist."

"Sheez," said the First Lady, "Sal was born in New Jersey, and Albericho isn't a Sicilian, he's a Neapolitan."

"Nevertheless." The single word was said as if it were a complete statement.

"Listen," said the Señora. "Is that a plane?"

"Yes," said Vásquez. "Air Force One. I recognize the sound."

From beyond the near hills, it now appeared, the single-engine Cessna that Vásquez called Air Force One, his private plane. It had picked up its passenger at one of Argentina's southernmost airports, after a chartered U.S.

44

jet had deposited him there. The Cessna landed, creating a fine spray of liquefied mud.

What now? was the question Kittering asked herself.

The first people out of the plane after the door opened were a couple of El Presidente's gunslingers, sent to Argentina to conduct Ricci safely back to La Calavera. They looked around cautiously, hands inside their bulging jackets, then spotted Vásquez and nodded to him. One of them turned and called inside the plane.

In a moment Vásquez had signaled Maestro Schütz, and the conductor had begun to lead the orchestra in the introductory measures to the welcoming aria. For from the plane had stepped a gray-haired man carrying a gift-wrapped hat box and dressed in the fitted pinstripe suit, silk shirt, silk tie, Borsalino hat, and wraparound sunglasses that were the unmistakable trademarks of Salvatore Ricci.

7

LUIGI Albericho began to sing, in tones as lush as black velvet:

"O tu, Palermo, terra adorata . . ."

The pinstriped figure walked slowly toward the welcoming committee as the Verdi melody embroidered the chill air of La Calavera's airstrip.

Vásquez smiled and waved. "Salvatore, my friend!"

The approaching figure waved back but did not speak.

Vásquez spoke to his wife. "It is good to see him, is it not? Dead, indeed!"

"Hey, wait a minute," said Señora Vásquez. "That's not Sal."

"What?" her husband said sharply. He looked at the visitor again and said through clenched teeth, "I believe you are right, my dear." Vásquez snapped out an order: *"Kill him!"*

"Wait!" cried Kittering, as the armed escorts pulled gleaming automatics from under their jackets and Espinoza's men looked to their general for orders.

"Wait?" snarled Vásquez. "Wait for what?"

The armed escorts, hesitant, held their fire. The visitor had stopped walking.

Kittering said, "You can always kill him, Señor. Why not wait and see who he is and why he's here?"

"She's right, Izzy," said the Señora. "If we keep him alive, that gives us *two* hostages."

Vásquez impatiently turned back to the visitor. "Who are you?" he angrily demanded.

The pinstriped man removed his Borsalino hat and dropped it to the ground. The sunglasses followed. Next he peeled off the wig of iron-gray hair and dropped it, too, into the mud of the landing strip.

"Name of Dodd," he said. "Are you Mr. Vásquez?"

"*¡Caramba!*" roared El Presidente. "Did you think to fool me with this masquerade?"

"No, sir," said Dodd. "I just wanted to make it as far as this island—and off the plane—alive, so I could talk to you."

"*Talk?* I want no *talk!*" The fuming, fulminating Vásquez walked up to Dodd and glared directly into his eyes. "I want Ricci! I was *promised* Ricci!"

"Understood," said Dodd. "That's why I brought him with me."

Vásquez blinked. "With you?"

"That's right."

"He is in the plane?"

"No, here he is."

Dodd opened the hat box, releasing a cloud of cold vapor.

"*¡Madre di Dios!*" cried El Presidente, looking inside.

"Izzy?" called his wife. "What is it?" She was walking toward them before Vásquez could stop her.

"No, no, my love, *do not look*, I implore you—"

But she was too fast, and Dodd could not replace the lid before she caught full sight of what was inside the box. Her olive skin went an exotic shade of off-ivory as she gasped for breath. "Sa—Sa—*Sally!*" she croaked. Her eyes rolled up into her head, her knees buckled, and she collapsed to the wet ground.

Vásquez bent over her as Dodd apologetically said,

"Sorry, Mr. Vásquez. I didn't mean for her to see this. It's not a pretty sight for a lady."

"Particularly not for the *sister* of Salvatore Ricci!" El Presidente said acidly.

Dodd inwardly cursed his chief for not mentioning that little detail. That his chief may not have known it he did not, at the moment, feel charitable enough to allow.

Luigi Albericho was still giving the full power of his mellifluous voice to the Verdi aria:

"Siciliani, ov' è il prisco valor? . . ."

Still on his knees next to his fallen wife, Vásquez shouted *"¡Silencio!"* to the basso, but he failed to hear the presidential injunction, due to the swelling of sound from the orchestra and from his own throat:

"Su, sorgete, sorgete a vittoria, all'onor! . . ."

"¡Silencio, silencio!" Vásquez screamed. But still Albericho sang on:

"O tu, Palermo . . ."

Enraged, Vásquez pulled a .45 Colt Commander automatic from a shoulder holster under his tailored jacket and fired three rounds into the operatic chest, instantly killing the singer.

A number of personal items were arranged in neat piles upon an antique seventeenth-century Spanish church altar that Ysidro Vásquez had purchased at an auction some years before and now used in his study as a kind of all-purpose workbench. He walked past the items slowly as the two gunslingers watched him with no little anxiety.

"Ricci's passport," El Presidente murmured in Spanish,

lifting that article and dropping it again. "Ricci's driver's license. Ricci's American Express card. Ricci's Blue Cross card. Ricci's wristwatch, engraved 'Happy Birthday, Sal. From your kid sister, Rosa Maria.' Ricci's suit. Ricci's hat. Ricci's shirt. Ricci's necktie. Only the shoes, the socks, and the underwear are not Ricci's."

"Also the wig," said the gunslinger who was not too scared to speak.

Vásquez nodded ominously, his eyes slits. "Tell me again, unspeakable pigs, how it comes to pass that you allow this, this, this DODD to come into my country impersonating the brother of my beloved wife, while all the time he is carrying the HEAD of the brother IN A BOX!!!"

Señora Vásquez, *née* Rosa Maria Ricci, was now abed and under sedation, on the advice of the presidential physician.

"Presidente," said the trembling henchman, "we had not ever seen Señor Ricci except for newspaper photographs. In that wig, hat, glasses, suit, this Dodd looked like him. We searched him, of course, with apologies, because we search everyone who comes to La Calavera. We would search our own mothers! He was unarmed. His passport and other identification was in order."

"You did not look in the BOX???"

"Oh, yes, Presidente. First we asked him what was in the box. He said, a gift for you: the head of a hated enemy. We look in the box. We see the vapors of dry ice and, through these, we see a head. It does not look to us like Señor Ricci, Presidente. The man in the hat looks more like Señor Ricci. Who are *we* to tell such a man that he cannot bring a head in a box to his brother-in-law?"

Vásquez smiled. The men smiled. Vásquez said, "I expect that you are both hungry. Do you like livers, sautéed with shallots and bacon?"

Both men nodded.

"Good!" screamed Vásquez. "Then I will personally cut out and sautée YOUR OWN LIVERS and feed them to you while you are still alive—if ever again you are responsible for the Señora suffering such an unpleasant experience! Do I make myself clear?"

They nodded their heads virtually off their shoulders.

"Very well. Now take me to the Dodd person."

"At once, Presidente. But may I suggest you put on a coat first? It is cold down there."

It was. Dodd was handcuffed to the refrigeration coils of El Presidente's soft drinks cellar. In view of the fact that all of his clothes, including shoes, socks, and underwear, were upstairs on the antique Spanish altar, he was stark naked. And almost literally blue. Vásquez was wrapped in a vicuña coat. His aides, in suits only, slapped and rubbed their arms.

"Now then, Mr. Dodd," said Vásquez, his breath forming puffs of condensation as he spoke, "if that is your true name. . . ."

"It-it is," Dodd said, his teeth chattering.

"How do I know that?"

"It's on my I.D."

"The only I.D. among your effects belongs to the late Salvatore Ricci. We even searched the shoes."

"Try the w-wig. Inside, under the lining."

"We will. But what, after all, will we find there? Something to tell us that you are an agent of United States law enforcement? The Central Intelligence Agency, perhaps? . . . Drug Enforcement Administration? . . ."

"FBI," said Dodd. He saw no need to open the temporary-resignation can of peas.

"My dear Dodd," said Vásquez pityingly, "you have no authority here. Do you know what we do with U.S. law enforcement agents?"

"Cut off their little f-f-fingers?"

50

"Among other things. Can you give me even one reason why we should not turn you into an ice sculpture?"

"Well," said the shivering Dodd, "l-l-let me see . . ."

"No need to hurry," Vásquez assured him. "You have plenty of time to, how do you say it, 'chill your heels'?"

Vásquez turned and began to walk out of the frosted cellar, followed by his two servitors.

"Wait," said Dodd. "I think my heels are ch-ch-chilled enough. Yes, I can give you a reason."

Vásquez turned again and faced Dodd. "I am listening."

Dodd shook his head. "For your ears only."

Vásquez shrugged. To the two men, he said in Spanish, "Wait upstairs."

They were glad to return to the warmth of El Presidente's private study. While they waited, they fingered the costly material of Ricci's pinstripe suit and silk shirt.

"This Dodd," said one to the other, "do you think he cut off Ricci's head himself?"

"How can one know?" replied his counterpart. "He is one brave fellow, coming here like this, unarmed, with that head in a box. I hate to say it of a stinking *yanqui* cop, but he is much man."

"He is!" agreed the other. "Did you note the size of his member?"

"Like a trench mortar!" observed his companion. "And in that cold! In such a temperature, mine would shrink to a dimple!"

Somewhat later Vásquez appeared in the study without his vicuña coat. Dodd was wearing it, and nothing else.

"There are your clothes, Mr. Dodd," said Vásquez. "But, first, a hot bath is called for, I think, and a hot drink. A tub of water will be drawn for you and mulled wine provided. You may keep the coat temporarily as a dressing gown. No doubt you will wish to rest after your long journey. You will be shown to your room after you have bathed. You will be called in plenty of time for dinner. Until then? . . ."

Dodd was conducted out of the study by the two men and his clothes—Ricci's clothes—carried away. Vásquez was left alone.

Soon the door opened again and his wife entered, clad in a robe and slippers. Her eyes were puffy, the pupils large, from weeping and the sedative drug.

She spoke in a hoarse whisper: "Where's my brother?"

"Beloved, please . . ."

"Where is he?"

"My dear, you are not rational. Salvatore is no more."

"I know that, damn it!" she snapped. "I mean, what have you done with his *head*? I want his *head*!"

"You do not want to see it, *mi corazón*."

"*Get it*."

With a sigh, Vásquez reached under the antique altar and brought the hat box into view. It remained cold to the touch from the vestiges of dry ice still inside. He placed it upon the altar and his wife lunged toward it, throwing off the lid. She thrust her hands into the vapor and lifted the gruesome, severed head of Ricci out of the box.

El Presidente shuddered. It was a ghastly scene out of Grand Guignol, out of *Salomé*, out of a B movie. "*Mi alma*," he moaned helplessly.

"Sally," she crooned to the head in her half-drugged state. She kissed the cold cheeks, the closed eyelids of the grisly object. "Whoever killed you," she said, "will pay, will suffer, will wish he was never born, will wish his mother, his grandmother, his great-grandmother were never born! I promise! You hear me, Sally? *I promise!*"

Vásquez inwardly told himself that it was as good as an Italian opera: *Si, vendetta! Tremenda vendetta!*

8

THE first chance Dodd had to talk to Kittering was as they were gathering for dinner, and that was a quickly muttered exchange behind false smiles.

"Dodd, what are you *doing* here?"

"Just follow my lead, don't contradict anything I may tell Vásquez, and if I should ask you, in his presence, to reveal something you may consider top secret—do it. And be sure you tell the truth."

"Like what?"

"Trust me. We are going to get off this island alive."

"I hope we can also string up that madman Vásquez by his sweetbreads," she said feelingly.

"Madman is right. Did you see what he did to that singer? And the Chief told me he's an opera buff! What are sweetbreads, exactly?"

"I've never been sure," said Kittering. "Shhh . . . here they come."

"Did I hear you discussing sweetbreads?" said Vásquez, walking up to them. "They are a favorite of mine. Perhaps tomorrow. But the entrée tonight is *biftek frite à la poulet*." He walked off.

"What the hell is that?" Dodd whispered.

"Chicken-fried steak," said Kittering.

At dinner Dodd, clad ghoulishly in Sal Ricci's pinstripe suit, silk shirt, and necktie, was seated between the First

53

Lady and Maestro Schütz. The lady said little during the soup course, but the Maestro had a great deal to say.

First, he corrected Dodd's pronunciation of his surname, explaining that it did not rhyme with the English words "cuts," "puts," or "boots," but, rather, was "Schütz, mit an umlaut." To Dodd's ear it sounded exactly like "Shits." The maestro then asked, "Are you a music lover, Herr Dodd?"

"I can carry a tune."

"Our host, the Presidente, is a true aficionado of the art. He insists upon the best. That is vy he engaged me. My reputation is known to you?"

"I'm not really into classics," Dodd admitted.

Schütz smiled bitterly. "You need not be diplomatic. My name is little known outside my native city, due to *prejudice!*" His voice rose sharply on the last word.

"Prejudice?" echoed Kittering, who was seated across the table. He nodded. "What is your native city?"

"Dachau," he replied.

Dodd choked on his soup.

"Have you ever visited my city, Fräulein?" Schütz asked Kittering. She shook her head. "Ach, it is *wunderbar!*" he assured her. "Fifteen miles north of Munich it lies, in Upper Bavaria. It is a city over tvelve hundred years old, mit a glorious history. I vould like to show it to you some time. Ve have many fine art exhibits, a vell-preserved Old City of great interest, a picturesque castle mit a view of the Alps, *und so weiter.* The population is not too large, not too small: about thirty-five thousand."

"Almost the same," said Kittering, "as the number of people who were killed there during the Hitler years."

"That vas only thirty-*two* thousand," Schütz said quickly. "And that happened not in the *city* of Dachau but in the camp nearby. But there, you see? Prejudice. It is the same alvays. Somebody sees the Dachau license plates on my automobile and slashes my tires! Tvelve hundred years of

German culture are forgotten and only the tvelve years of that camp are remembered! Oh, I tell you, Fräulein, sometimes it makes me *so mad!*"

He bent the soup spoon double in his white-knuckled fists.

"Calm yourself, my dear Ottokar," said Vásquez from the other end of the table. "You are among friends."

Schütz nodded to his host and—Dodd could have sworn—managed to click his heels, even while seated. He turned to Dodd. "I organized and trained a magnificent group of musicians and called the group the Dachau Symphony Orchestra. How proud my city vas of me! Ve vere invited to play on television in Munich. So excited ve vere! But the announcer refused to call us the Dachau Symphony Orchestra. He suggested ve change the name to the Upper Bavaria Symphony Orchestra! Vot?? Change??? A name tvelve hundred years old??? Never! Ve packed up and returned to Dachau mitout playing on television. It vas . . . humiliating, discouraging. That is vy I accepted our host's offer." He caught the eye of Vásquez. *"Mein Präsident?"* he inquired. "Vot shall ve do for a basso now?"

"I will telephone to Italy tomorrow," said Vásquez, "and begin negotiations for a replacement. I am inclining toward Rinaldi. What do you think?"

Schütz smiled. "As usual, *mein Präsident*, your taste is exquisite."

"Miss Kittering," said Vásquez, "would you care for more Fresca?"

"No, thank you, Señor."

"You, Mr. Dodd?"

Rosa Maria Vásquez, with a sidelong look at Dodd, said to her husband, "Maybe our guests would rather have wine." She lifted her own glass of white wine to her lips.

"I'm fine, really," said Dodd.

"This is *vintage* Fresca," Vásquez pointed out.

"Vintage?" said Kittering.

"Yes, indeed," he said proudly. "Early January 1980. Just slightly later in that year the company began to market a different beverage under the same name."

"I thought they just changed the can," said Dodd.

"That is what most people thought," said El Presidente. "I remember their television commercials of the period. I was visiting your country at the time. 'Take your last look at good old Fresca,' they said, and a pair of disembodied hands ripped the old familiar label from the can, revealing the new design beneath. But it was not only the design that was changed, it was the drink itself. I sampled the new Fresca, of course. It tasted and even *looked* completely different from the old. In my judgment, it was no more than a poor imitation of Fresca's chief competitor, Diet 7-Up. I like 7-Up, but I also like Fresca—the *old* Fresca. So I bought up several hundred cases of the old—all I could find in your markets—and had them shipped down here." He lifted his glass. "You are drinking it now."

Dodd eyed his own glass as if it were a beaker of urine specimen. "Awesome," he said.

"I wrote to the president of the company, saying, 'The true Fresca is being usurped by an imposter with the same name, bearing no resemblance to the original.'"

Kittering asked, "Did you get a reply?"

"In the fullness of time," said Vásquez, "and not from the president but from a public relations specialist. It was full of, how do you call it, 'soft soup'? He wrote, 'It is consumers like you who make our business truly worthwhile. That is why it concerns us greatly that you did not find new Fresca acceptable.' He then assured me that the reformulation was a direct result of 'consumer input,' and, to help me 'get reacquainted' with their product, he enclosed a coupon good for a free six-pack of the bogus Fresca."

"Impertinence!" snapped Maestro Schütz.

"Naturally, I returned the coupon," said Vásquez. "And I will savor my dwindling supply of the genuine beverage for as long as it lasts. Unfortunately, there is no 'Fresca Classic' in response to 'huge demand.' Just my one little voice, crying in the wilderness." He sighed and sipped from his glass.

Wind howled past the windows and rain punished the roof. Rosa Maria rolled her eyes in resignation. But Vásquez assured his guests: "This is nothing. We are in the path of cyclones here, and when they are on the rampage, ah, *then* there is cause for concern."

After the last course Vásquez announced that four members of the orchestra's string section would play quartets for them in the music room.

"What?" yelped the First Lady. "I thought we were going to see a Clint Eastwood movie!"

"The Señora," explained Vásquez with a smile, "is a devotée of the American *film noir*. But, my dear, the Clint Eastwood picture did not arrive as promised. We were sent a Mexican vampire film by mistake. The careless ones will be punished, have no fear."

Rosa Maria grumbled, "I'd rather watch the Mexican vampire movie than listen to fiddlers."

"Come, come, *querida*, you are joking. We cannot subject our guests to such disgusting rubbish." He rose from the table. "Ladies, gentlemen: coffee and cognac will be served in the music room in ten minutes. We will assemble there."

In the interim, while they strolled between dining room and music room under the watchful eyes of El Presidente's security guards, Dodd and Kittering were able to hold a muted conversation.

"Maestro Shits is a bigger flake than Vásquez," Dodd observed.

Kittering nodded. "I tried to get a reaction from him before dinner about the way Vásquez gunned down the basso. Know what he said? 'One Italian more or less is of no importance. An inferior race. Oh, they can *sing*, but . . .'"

"He better not let Mrs. Vásquez hear him say that."

"He won't," said Kittering. "He may be crazy, but he's not stupid. He knows which side his *Gänseleberpastete-schnitte* is buttered on."

"His what?"

"*Paté de foie gras.* That's what you were eating as an appetizer tonight."

"I thought it was liver sausage."

"It is." Dropping her voice even lower, she asked, "Do they know you're the one who killed Ricci?"

"No," said Dodd.

"What's your game plan?"

"Too hard to talk now," he muttered. "When the Chief told me you were down here minus a piece of your finger, I knew I had to think fast . . . do something . . . anything . . . so I got carte blanche to do whatever I wanted with Ricci's effects—clothes, passport, and so on—and his corpse. I got the pathologists to pack his head in dry ice. And then I just winged it."

"Like you winged it in Vegas."

"Well, that didn't turn out too bad, did it? I broke up the Ricci mob and came away with damn near half a million bucks."

"And almost got yourself nailed by Farnsworth. I had to save your ass."

"Maybe that's why I'm here. To return the favor and save yours. It happens to be my favorite ass." Half a second later he added, "Next to mine."

Two violinists, a violist, and a cellist, all in evening dress, were already seated at four spindly music stands. Dodd, when he and Kittering entered the music room, was struck by the grim facial expressions of the four musicians. He didn't like to think in terms of ethnic stereotype, but they reminded him of nothing so much as those archive newsreels of defendants at the Nuremberg war crimes trials. It became clear that, when Schütz had come to La Calavera, he had brought the Dachau Symphony Orchestra with him, lock, stock, and glockenspiel.

Vásquez smiled grandly at his guests. "There is a prepared program, of course," he said, "but I am assured that the musicians have an extensive repertoire and would welcome any requests."

Kittering said, "In that case, how about one of the string quartets of Mendelssohn?"

All four of the players turned their heads in her direction at the same time and stared coldly at her.

Schütz barked, "Mendelssohn? The Jew?"

"Felix Mendelssohn, that's right. Any one of his quartets would be fine. He wrote seven of them, I think."

"I am sorry," Schütz said primly. "Ve have not any vorks by that person in our repertoire. Ve vill perform Beethoven." He nodded curtly to the four string players and they began sawing away obediently.

Halfway through the first movement, Rosa Maria Vásquez leaned toward Dodd and murmured in his ear, "A little of this goes a long way. See you later. . . ." She slipped quietly from the room.

After the musicale, Vásquez said to Dodd and Kittering, "It is late and this has been a tiring day. I suggest we postpone our discussion of business matters until tomorrow."

The Americans were conducted to their separate suites.

When Dodd walked into the bedroom of his suite, he was startled to find Rosa Maria Vásquez sitting on the bed in a pink satin negligée that was approximately as opaque as Handi-Wrap. Her prominent nipples and dark areolas intimidated him like a pair of pistol barrels.

"So how was the concert?" she asked.

"Oh, you know," he replied. "You heard one string quartet, you heard them all."

Señora Vásquez stood up. She untied the sash of her negligée and shrugged the sheer garment off her shoulders. It trickled off her nude body like spring water to become a satin puddle at her feet. Her burnished skin was sleek and reflective, shimmering in the half light of the muted lamp. She was a classic Italian sculpture of perfectly placed globes, curves, hemispheres, molded in warmblooded flesh.

"Holy Socks," said Dodd, "you are *some* kind of greatlooking lady, Mrs. Vásquez."

"Aw, don't call me Mrs. Vásquez," she wheedled, stepping closer to him. "Call me Rosa Maria." She ran her hands up and down him.

"That's kind of long," he said.

"So is this," she chuckled, holding on to him for dear life. "But I'm not complaining."

"How about I call you Rosa?" he croaked.

"Sure, call me Rosa. Hold me and call me Rosa. I'm going off my rocker on this island. I'm a passionate woman and I need a man, a real man, understand?"

Dodd nodded. "What about El Presidente?"

"Izzy?" she said scornfully. "My brother married me off to him for business reasons. He's too old for me."

"He's what, about forty-five?" said Dodd. "That's not so old. And he's got all that Latin charm."

"Oh, Latin charm he's got," she conceded. "He could sell it in jars like peanut butter, he's got so much of it, but that's not what I want, what I need, what I'm dying for. . . . Hey, Sal's suit is a little small on you, isn't it?" She had been undressing Dodd as she talked, and now he stood naked except for his shoes. "The son of a bitch is queer," she added.

"Oh?"

"Queer for women."

"Oh?"

"You know, that French stuff. But a woman wants a real screw from a real man, know what I mean?"

"Sure, Rosa. Sure I do."

"Then what are you waiting for?"

"Just want to take off my shoes."

"Fuck the shoes. Leave them on! *Take* me, big guy! Take me *now!*"

Dodd did not disappoint her.

When she had had her squealing, gasping, thrashing, gnashing fill of him, and he had thrown himself on his back next to her, covered by a gleaming clear varnish of sweat, she let the fingers of her left hand toy with him, while her right hand reached down to the negligée that lay crumpled on the floor next to the bed. She extracted something from the pocket as her left hand cupped that precious part of Dodd sometimes referred to whimsically as the family jewels.

"Hey, what the hell!" Dodd said suddenly. "That's *cold!* What have you got there?"

"A razor, big fella," she replied softly. "An old-fashioned barber-shop straight razor. My brother gave it to me when I started high school—to defend my honor, he said. He didn't know I'd been screwing since I was twelve. But I kept it in my purse anyway, for muggers, you know?"

"Good idea," Dodd said faintly. "But why have you got it out now, Rosa?"

"Because you are going to tell me who killed my brother," she said, touching the blunt edge of the blade to his jewels. "If you don't, you're going to be singing coloratura in my husband's opera company."

"I'm not really into classics," said Dodd.

9

EARLIER that same day, Mrs. Rudnick had been having a midmorning break in her favorite coffeeshop. It called itself a tearoom, but she called it a coffeeshop. The other regulars all knew Mrs. Rudnick at sight and by name, but weren't sure if she was a married woman, widowed, or divorced. She was a trim, bird-bright person of sixty.

"Audrey," she said to the woman behind the counter, "let me have a cheese Danish."

"The cheese are all gone, Mrs. Rudnick. How about prune?"

"I hate prune."

"How about a croissant?"

"Hey, I *really* hate those phony French things. The young couples in my building are always shoving them in their kissers. Croissants for breakfast, croissants for lunch, croissants for tea . . . they're croissanting themselves straight into the boneyard, if you ask me. If they laid off the croissants, they wouldn't have to jog so much."

"How about a jelly doughnut?"

Mrs. Rudnick sighed. "You twisted my arm." When Audrey brought the greasy, sugar-covered fritter, Mrs. Rudnick said, "You know what we used to call these things in Chicago? Maybe they still do. Bismarcks."

"Dumb name," said Audrey.

"I guess it is, but the first time I came here to New York

and somebody offered me a jelly doughnut, I didn't know what they meant."

Mrs. Rudnick opened her newspaper to the television listings. "No two ways about it, Audrey," she said. "I'm just going to have to get myself one of those VCR things. The stuff they're putting out on the nets I wouldn't feed to a dog."

A very young man at the other end of the counter sighed heavily as he sorted through a handful of glossy brochures.

"Who's he?" Mrs. Rudnick asked in a low voice.

Audrey shrugged. "Never saw him before."

"Kind of cute."

"A little too young for us, though."

"Speak for yourself," said Mrs. Rudnick. "What's all that stuff he's looking at?"

"Travel folders," said Audrey. "Can't seem to make up his mind." Audrey sauntered off to take care of another customer.

Mrs. Rudnick, raising her voice, addressed the prospective traveler: "Going someplace?"

He looked up at her. "Beg pardon?"

"Those folders. Planning a trip?"

He shrugged. "Supposed to be. Thing is, where?"

"Depends on—" Mrs. Rudnick picked up her jelly doughnut and coffee and moved to the stool next to him. "Mind if I join you?" He shook his head. "Depends on the kind of thing you like and where you've already been. Also how much time you got, and how much money."

"Two weeks," he said, "and not much money at all. But I'd like it to be nice, something we can remember . . ."

"Don't tell me!" said Mrs. Rudnick. "It's a honeymoon!"

"That's right. We're getting married on Friday."

"Well, congratulations! And you still don't know where you're going to honeymoon?"

"Just can't seem to decide."

"Hey, I'm an expert on honeymoons! I could write a book on them!"

"Really? How many have you had?"

"Who's counting? I always had a great time, though. But who doesn't? On honeymoons, know what I mean?"

"Right," he said with a grin. "What places would you recommend? Where have you been?"

"Well, gee, the first marriage we didn't go anywhere at all, couldn't afford it, too poor, just stayed home, but we had a great time, anyway. We were just a couple of kids. Then, with my second husband, Mr. Dodd, I went to Hawaii . . ."

"Hawaii, huh?"

An alarm went off in Mrs. Rudnick's head. "No, hold the phone. Hawaii was my *third* husband. Mr. Dodd and I honeymooned in Fargo."

"Fargo?"

"That's right. Fargo, South Dakota."

"North Dakota."

"North, South . . . listen, it could have been *East* Dakota, for all I knew! I was on my honeymoon, not studying geography. We stayed at the Powers Hotel. I wonder if it's still there? . . ."

"Nice place?"

"All I saw was the ceiling, sonny. Hey, you're *blush*ing!" She slid her small bottom off the stool, gathered up her purse and newspaper, and drained her coffee cup. "Ah, good to the last drop," she said. "Nice talking to you. *Fargo.* Go for it. Something different. Your bride will never forget it."

Later, as he left the coffeshop, Special Agent Farnsworth dumped the travel folders into a convenient trash bin. Then he hailed a cab, went straight to Kennedy, and took the next jet back to Washington.

* * *

"Start talking," Rosa Maria Vásquez commanded.

"First of all," said Dodd in the bed beside her, "I want to apologize for bringing that hat box here. Really tacky. No class. But I didn't know there'd be any close relatives of Sal Ricci here, like his sister, honest. And I couldn't think of any other way to make your husband believe that Sal was dead. Photos of the body? Too easy to fake. It was the only thing I could come up with."

"Did you kill him?" she asked fiercely, and Dodd felt the flat side of the razor against his delicate parts.

"*Me?* Of course not! I loved the guy! He was my *padrone!*"

"Your—" Rosa Maria's mouth fell open. "What the hell are you talking about? The FBI is your *padrone!*"

"The Bureau is my *cover*, Rosa," he said slowly, as if explaining to a child. "Long before I ever worked for the Bureau, I was a New York cop, on the Ricci payroll."

"That's a load of crap. I never heard of you before."

"Well, we didn't exactly hold a press conference and invite the reporters. It was supposed to be our little secret."

"You lying bastard! *You* killed him!"

"No! Cross my heart! I almost *got* killed, trying to save his life!"

"*What?*"

Dodd sighed. "Look. It was like this. I was in Vegas on business. Your brother's business. I went out to his house to talk to him. Also to pick up some small change to use for payoffs. You know, bribes."

"How much small change?" she asked suspiciously.

"Four hundred long ones. Sal knew he could trust me with it. He always let me handle that sort of thing. Anyway—"

"Hold it!" Rosa Maria said sharply. "Sal had a lot of cops on the pad, sure, but he never would have trusted four hundred yards in cash to an egg-salad sandwich like you. Only a goombah rated that kind of trust."

"So what do I look like, Chinese?"

"You look like what you are, a Dodd. Dodd: what the hell kind of name is that?"

"English, I guess. Scotch-Irish, I don't know. It was my dad's name, may he rest in peace. But my mother's maiden name was Lazzarelli."

"No shit."

"Hey," said Dodd, "I don't mess around with my mother's name. It's sacred, know what I mean?"

"So your old lady had an Italian name, so what?"

"So nothing. So that's how I got to know your brother, through my mother's side of the family, my Uncle Tonio. He introduced us. Sal—Mr. Ricci I used to call him then— took a liking to me for some reason. Treated me like a son. I looked up to him. He was a wonderful man, like a second father. You must have looked up to him, too. I guess he was a lot older than you, huh?"

"Twenty years," Rosa Maria said softly. "I was the baby of the family. Now quit stalling and tell me who killed him."

"As I was saying," Dodd continued, "I went to his house in Vegas for a business meeting and to pick up that money. Well, we talk, we drink a little wine—"

"What kind of wine?" Rosa Maria demanded suddenly.

"How should I know? Wine, that's all. Careful with that razor, will you?"

"Red or white?"

Dodd felt that the fate of his manhood depended on his answer. He remembered her glass that evening at dinner. She had sipped the same wine all through the meal. Maybe that was the way to go.

"White," he replied.

She relaxed. "Corvo di Salaparuta," she said, "from

Sicily. It's the only wine he ever drank. The only wine I drink, too. Go on."

"Well, your brother opens the safe and gets the money. But this chock-full-o'-nuts Mario—"

"Mario Fontana?"

"That's the one. I figure the dice he's shooting craps with got no dots on them, because as soon as he sees all that nice crisp romaine, he snaps and pulls out a forty-five. Now, I'm not carrying. *Nobody* goes into Sal's house packing heat. So when this Mario waves me back, I back off. But not your brother! Hey, that was one tough guy! He *goes* for Mario! I yell 'Don't, Sal!' I try to throw myself between Sal and Mario, but your brother pushes me aside and tries to jump Mario—"

Dodd broke off.

"Then what?" asked Rosa Maria.

"Well . . . that's all there is," Dodd said lamely. "Mario shot him. One round and it was all over. He—he didn't suffer, Rosa."

"And what happened to that bastard, Mario?"

"He tried to perforate *me* next. I went for him, same as Sal, but I had better luck—younger than Sal, maybe that's why—got hold of the gun and plugged him."

"Mario Fontana!" growled Rosa Maria. "I never did like that son of a bitch! He was always grabbing my ass, even when I was ten years old. I always thought Sally was wrong to trust him—and it turns out I was right. But I'm sorry you killed him."

"You are?"

"Yeah. I wish I had him here. *Alive.* . . ." She gripped the razor meaningfully.

"Rosa," Dodd requested in a faint voice, "would you mind putting that thing down now?"

She closed the razor carefully and dropped it to the floor. "So what did you do then?"

"What *could* I do? There I was, an FBI Agent with two

dead underworld figures on the floor in front of me. I could have just split, but I figured—why not use this to make myself a big hero with the Bureau and therefore all the more useful to the organization? Which is what I did."

"What happened to the money?"

"I stashed it—partly because it might have looked funny to the Bureau if four hundred grand was sitting there in the middle of the room between the two bodies, 'just happened' to be there while I was making a collar. And partly because I knew I'd be needing it to make those payoffs. The show must go on, right? Your brother would have wanted it that way."

"I see. Stashed it where?"

"Ah," said Dodd. "I'm keeping that little piece of information as a bargaining chip to use when I do business with your husband tomorrow. Besides, I don't want to talk anymore."

"Why not?"

"Something's come up," he said tenderly.

10

A T breakfast the following morning, a meal that
    included kedgeree, kidneys, and kippers, in addi-
    tion to more conventional American dishes such as
bacon and eggs, El Presidente insisted on airing the
problems of his opera company to an unresponsive, even
unsympathetic, audience consisting of his wife, Kittering,
and Dodd.

"It is not only that I must find a replacement for the
basso Albericho," he explained, "but I may also lose my
leading tenor, Montini."

"Why, did you shoot him, too?" asked Rosa Maria.

"No, my dove. But he is livid with anger at Maestro
Schütz and may refuse to work with him. I cannot say that
I blame him. Schütz is a great conductor, but he has
treated Montini abominably."

"What did he do?" asked Dodd, struggling with a
kipper.

"He cut out Montini's cabalettas."

"He *did?*" said Dodd, shocked by a mental picture of
Rosa Maria's razor.

"He most certainly did. Cut them right out." After a
moment Vásquez added, "Both of them."

"Why would Shits do . . . a thing a like that?" Dodd
inquired.

"Because he's a cold, unfeeling man."

"But . . ." Dodd hesitated. "This Montini must be in a bad way."

"He is ill."

"I should think so! Will he ever be able to—well—you know—"

"Able to what?"

"Well—among other things—*sing*," said Dodd.

"Not with the same enthusiasm," Vásquez replied.

"You're not going to let Shits get away with it, are you?"

"What is to stop him?"

"Why . . . the law? Even in a place like this . . ."

Vásquez smiled. "I agree, Mr. Dodd. There *ought* to be a law against such things. 'Even in a place like this.' But there is not."

Dodd was almost, but not quite, speechless. "But . . . mutilation? . . . grievous bodily harm? . . . "

Vásquez looked at him curiously. "What on earth are you talking about?"

"Montini's cabalettas."

"What about them?"

"Izzy," said Señora Vásquez, "what the hell *are* cabalettas, anyway?"

Vásquez sighed. "A cabaletta," he said patiently, "is the second movement of the old-fashioned Italian aria. Montini has rousing cabalettas in two of his arias this season, one in *Rigoletto*, another in *La Traviata*. Sometimes conductors have been known to cut out a cabaletta to speed up a performance, although true opera lovers disapprove. Schütz has cut out *both* of Montini's. It has made him positively ill. But, of course, I must not interfere with the maestro's prerogative."

"Of course not," said Dodd, giving up on the kipper.

"And now," Vásquez said briskly, putting down his napkin, "if the ladies will excuse us, we will discuss business matters, Mr. Dodd."

"Why not let them stay?" Dodd suggested. "The Señora

is the sister of my late *padrone*, and I have no secrets from her."

"Very well, if you wish, but—"

"And Field Investigator Kittering is part of the Ricci organization, same as I am."

"What?" Señor and Señora Vásquez bleated in unison.

Kittering nodded, although she was every bit as dazed by Dodd's statement as El Presidente and his wife.

"But why did you not tell me that before?" Vásquez asked her.

"Would you have believed me?" she responded.

"I don't believe it *now!*" snapped Rosa Maria, turning to Dodd. "What kind of cheap trick are you trying to pull? I was just barely able to swallow your story about working for my brother, being trusted with four hundred G's and all that. *Just barely.* Now you try to tell us that this Justice Department twat worked for him, *too?*"

Dodd smiled. "I don't blame you, Señora, but facts are facts. Kittering and I both worked for Sal, and he trusted both of us. In fact, I trusted her so much that I let her do the actual stashing of that money. I even told her not to tell me where she stashed it, so that I couldn't possibly reveal it, under any kind of pressure. As of this very moment, I don't know where it is. But Miss Kittering does." He turned to her. "Don't you?"

Don't contradict anything I tell Vásquez, Dodd had warned her. So she replied, "Yes, I do."

"Where is it?" asked Vásquez.

"Ah," said Dodd with a chuckle, "not so fast, Presidente. The way I see it, that money is our ticket out of here—Miss Kittering's and mine."

"Are you afraid I will steal it?" said Vásquez, insulted.

"Of course not!" said Dodd. "You're a man of honor. Besides, what's four hundred thousand dollars to you? Chicken feed. No, but if you send somebody to find that money—and if it's where Miss Kittering says it is—that will *prove* that I've been telling the truth about our connection with your late brother-in-law."

"Oh, yeah?" snarled Rosa Maria. "All it'll prove is that she's got four hundred large in her piggy bank! Like you said, chicken feed."

"No, *querida*," said her husband, "not quite. To us, undoubtedly, such a sum is chicken's food, but to persons of relatively modest means, law enforcement agents, we must admit that it would be of greater significance."

"I still say it doesn't prove a thing!" Rosa Maria insisted.

Kittering leaned forward. "The Señora is right," she said, "or she would be right if the money was just *any* four hundred thousand dollars. But it isn't. It's Ricci money, from a Ricci casino—"

"Hey, I get it!" Rosa Maria said quickly. "You mean the bills are marked?"

Kittering smiled. "And you know exactly in what *way* Ricci money is marked, don't you, Señora?"

"You bet I do! A little invisible 'R' that shows up only in special light—ultraviolet or infrared, I forget which. Discourages skimming."

"And this money," asked Vásquez, "is all marked in such a manner? All four hundred thousand dollars?"

"If you were Salvatore Ricci, Señor," said Kittering, "wouldn't you make sure that every one of those bills was marked?"

Vásquez shrugged.

"Okay, then," Dodd said quickly. "Once you've checked out the marked money and established that we're all on the same team, we'll have a basis for further negotiation."

"Negotiation?" echoed Vásquez.

"Well, you know," said Dodd, "I'd like to make a pitch for taking over Sal Ricci's territory in the States, become your U.S. partner, same as he was."

"Hey, wait a minute—" Rosa Maria began.

But Dodd cut in with "First things first, however. Have you thought about who you'll send to check out the money, Señor? Which one of your men do you trust that much? Two-fifths of a million is quite a temptation."

Vásquez nodded. "True. But that is my concern."

"Pardon me, but it's my concern, too. That money was entrusted to me by the Señora's brother. I'm sworn to use it only in a specific way. If I allow it to be stolen, and the organization—*our* organization—fails to run smoothly because certain payoffs aren't made, I'm responsible. So before Miss Kittering tells us where she hid it, I want to make certain I agree with your choice of . . . uh . . . courier."

Vásquez sighed. "Let us have some more coffee." He rang for the servant, who brought an urn of fresh, steaming coffee, and filled the cups of the Señora, Kittering, and Dodd. Then he poured Dr. Pepper into El Presidente's goblet.

"Fool!" screamed Vásquez, dashing the bottle from the servant's hand. "I am drinking Shasta Tiki Punch this morning!"

Begging forgiveness, the trembling man picked up the fallen bottle and backed out of the room.

"I have decided," said Vásquez at last. "I will look into the matter of the money myself."

"Izzy, are you nuts?" cried Rosa Maria. "That's exactly what these two want—don't you see that? What becomes of La Calavera if the strong man, El Presidente, just takes off for the States, leaving a pair of Federal goons here? Everything would fall apart! And is there anything the DEA would like better than Ysidro Vásquez, the Cocaine King, walking into their spiderweb?"

Vásquez smiled. "They have no evidence against me in the United States, my beloved. They may suspect much, but they have no proof, nothing conclusive to connect me with my American partners. They cannot arrest me, unless I were foolish enough to carry drugs into their country on my person!"

"What about kidnapping the lady cop? They could grab you for that!"

He frowned. "You may have a point, even though I have diplomatic immunity as a head of state. . . ."

"I wouldn't bet the farm on that, Izzy. This cockamamie chunk of rock a *state*? To you it's a state. To the poor suckers who call you Presidente, it's a state. But to the good old U.S.A., is it a state?"

Vásquez muttered, "There is, admittedly, some difference of opinion about that . . . but, *querida*, who else can I send on such a mission? Who can I trust?"

"*Me*," said Rosa Maria, jabbing a thumb deep between her breasts.

"You, my dove? But you are a member of the notorious Ricci family. . . ."

"So what? They can't arrest *me*. I don't have a record. I'm clean. I've got a valid passport. I can parade my ass in and out of the country till it falls off."

"I do not know, my love. I dislike sending you into danger."

"What danger? Traffic? Smog? I'm in more danger down here from cyclones. What is it, Izzy, *don't you trust me?*" The tone of her voice struck terror to the soul of El Presidente.

"Of course I trust you, *querida*."

"Then it's settled. Okay with you, Dodd? After all, it's my brother's money, and I'm his closest living relative, so in a way it's my money now."

Dodd shrugged. "Sure."

Rosa Maria turned to Kittering. "So where did you stash it, honey?"

Kittering hesitated.

74

"Go ahead," said Dodd. "Tell her."

If I should ask you to reveal something you may consider top secret, Dodd had urged her, *do it, and be sure you tell the truth.*

"All right," said Kittering. "I mailed it to myself."

"Huh?" Dodd grunted.

"I made a big package out of it, marked it 'Books,' and sent it off by fourth-class mail. You know how long *that* can take."

"When did you mail it?" Dodd asked.

"Just before the Presidente's men abducted me. I had just returned to my apartment from the mailbox, and they were waiting for me inside, with their chloroform all ready. Next stop, La Calavera!"

"So the money," said Dodd, "is probably still en route in the mail?"

Kittering nodded.

"But eventually," said Vásquez, "it will be delivered to your home, your apartment?"

"No," she replied. "To my post office box."

"Okay," Rosa Maria said impatiently, "where's the p.o. box key?"

"I gave it to someone."

"Who?" asked Dodd.

"Farnsie."

"*What?*" Dodd yelped.

"Who the hell is Farnsie?" Rosa Maria demanded.

"Someone Dodd and I know."

"Why did you give it to *him?*" Dodd wailed.

"I didn't exactly *give* it to him," Kittering explained. "I planted it on him. He doesn't know he has it."

Dodd groaned.

"Please elucidate, Señorita," El Presidente said with a sigh.

"Well," said Kittering, after taking a deep breath, "first I had to make a play for him. Date him. He took me to dinner, then we went back to his place for a drink. And . . . you know." She avoided Dodd's eyes.

"Boy oh boy," mumbled Dodd.

"Well, he's kind of cute!" she said defensively.

"Please continue," said Vásquez.

"Then . . . afterward . . . I asked him if I could use his shower. Of course he said I could, and that's when I got a real break. He told me he never took a shower."

"You mean the son of a bitch is filthy?" said Rosa Maria.

"No, he prefers bathtubs. So the shower stall in his bathroom hadn't been used the whole time he'd been renting the place. 'I hope it works,' he said. I told him I'd risk it, and I did. The water came out a little rusty at first, but I didn't mind. After my shower, I used some adhesive tape from his medicine cabinet and taped my p.o. box key to the top of the metal frame of the shower door. The one thing he never uses. He'll never see it there."

Dodd said, "But how did you plan to get it back?"

Kittering merely looked at him pityingly.

"And how," said Vásquez, "will the Señora be able to get it?"

Rosa Maria looked at *him* pityingly.

"But, my dear one—"

"Don't worry, Izzy, I won't bend your Latin honor out of shape. I won't go all the way."

Vásquez shook his head mournfully. "I do not know, *querida*. It is not to my liking. Flirting with a strange man, going to his apartment, leading him on, inflaming his passions . . . what if he should overcome you and take advantage of you?"

"I can handle it."

"*No!*" cried Vásquez, suddenly springing to his feet. He indicated Dodd and Kittering with an imperious sweep of the hand, saying, "Why are we wasting time listening to them? Why should we care if they are telling the truth or not? What does it matter? Let the money sit in the post office box. We do not need it. We do not need *them*. They have outlived their usefulness." He shouted: *"Hombres!"*

Through two different doors, two men simultaneously exploded into the room. In their hands were Uzi fully automatic weapons.

11

"DON'T be stupid, Vásquez," said Dodd. "If you kill us, you're in big trouble."

Vásquez snarled wordlessly and motioned to his men.

"Not here, Izzy!" Rosa Maria demanded. "Not in the house!"

"Of course not, my dear." He instructed his men, in Spanish, to remove the two American guests from the house before dispatching them.

"Big trouble, I'm telling you," Dodd repeated. "You had Investigator Kittering less than forty-eight hours and they sent me down here to bail her out. If both of us disappear, can you imagine the kind of visitors you'll get from the U.S. of A.? The Marines."

Vásquez laughed. "I think not, Mr. Dodd. How long were those Americans held hostage in Iran before that failed attempt was made to rescue them? Over five months, was it not? And there were fifty-two of them. There are only two of you. I think you overestimate your importance."

"I think you *under*estimate our importance—to Sal Ricci. And to you."

"Enough of this talk," said Vásquez, and motioned again to his men.

"Wait a minute," said Rosa Maria. "What do you mean, your importance to Sal?"

78

"Your brother," said Dodd, "had a network of vital contacts all over the States, from coast to coast. None of them knew each other, but each one of them knew Sal, and Sal knew them—by heart. He had their names, addresses, phone numbers *memorized*."

"He did?" said Rosa Maria.

Dodd nodded. "Never wrote them down, so they could never fall into the wrong hands—like the law, or competitors. That's why your husband is afraid his whole U.S. operation is going to fall apart, now that Sal is dead."

"I am?" said Vásquez, blinking.

"You'd better be, Presidente."

"Yeah, so?" said Rosa Maria.

"So—maybe it was caution, maybe it was a premonition, I don't know—but when Sal handed me that money, he told me that he was also handing over the list of names and addresses. He had written them down for the first time, and they were wrapped up with the money. I think that's what made Mario go bonkers. It wasn't just the four hundred long johns, it was the list of names, the key to the whole Ricci operation. Sal was giving it to me, not to him, to *me*, and I'm not even a full-blooded goombah. He blew a fuse. Mario figured, if he could knock off Sal and me *and* get hold of that list, he'd be king of the hill. The whole country would have to do business with *him*. But, as it turned out, the whole country will have to do business with *me*." Dodd smiled at Vásquez. "So will you, Presidente."

Vásquez said nothing for a moment. His lips narrowed. Then his eyes narrowed. Then his nostrils widened. "This so-called list, where is it now?"

"Where it's always been. Where Sal put it. With the money. Wrapped up inside one of the stacks of bills."

"In a post office box in Washington?"

"Right."

To Kittering, Vásquez said, "And the key to the box is hidden in the apartment of this . . . Farnsie?"

She nodded.

"Who is Farnsie?"

"Well, now," said Dodd, "if you kill us, that's something you'll never find out."

"True," Vásquez conceded. "But fingertips can be removed *without* anesthetic, too."

"So can other things," Rosa Maria added darkly.

"That takes time, though," said Dodd. "There's already a dangerous power vacuum in the U.S. branch of your operation. With the information I can give you—that list, and so on—you can plug the leak right away. Presto, business as usual. No fuss, no muss. And you'd have two employees who are also direct pipelines to federal law enforcement! You'd be crazy to pass up a deal like that."

"He's right, Izzy," said Rosa Maria. "Back to Plan One. They tell us who Farnsie is and where we find him, I go Stateside and bring home the bacon."

Vásquez hesitated. "I do not like it, but . . . very well." He motioned the two men out of the room. "Now tell us who this Farnsie is."

Dodd tsk-tsked. "But you won't respect us any more, after you've taken our cherry. What do you think we use for brains—Campbell's Cream of Mushroom Soup? No way, José. We need insurance."

"You are in *no position to bargain!*" Vásquez screamed.

"Really? I thought we were."

Rosa Maria asked, "What kind of insurance?"

"I was thinking something like this," said Dodd. "Instead of you going to Washington alone, you go with Kittering. Each of you keeps an eye on the other. I stay here, as a hostage." He turned to Vásquez. "That way your wife won't have to make a play for Farnsie. Kittering will do a repeat performance, get her key back, both ladies will open the p.o. box, and come back here with the goodies."

"A minute ago," said Rosa Maria, "you were all in favor of me going alone. Why the switch?"

"No switch," Dodd assured her, "just a little embroidery. I'm looking for a way to make your trip more acceptable to your husband. He's against the idea of you—what did you call it, Presidente?—inflaming Farnsie's passions. But you can't have any objections to Investigator Kittering inflaming Farnsie. After all, she's already inflamed him."

"Izzy," the First Lady snapped, "a word with you. . . ." She motioned him to a far corner of the room where they could hold a muttered conversation.

Kittering took advantage of this to hold a similar conference with Dodd. "You knew she'd jump at the chance to get back to the States, didn't you?" she whispered.

"I was hoping she would, if I opened the door wide enough for her, but I wanted the idea to come from her, not from me. My impression is she's had it up to here with him and with this island."

"I didn't see any list tucked away with that money. You made that up, didn't you?"

"Of course! On the spur of the moment, to save our necks."

"Do you ever tell the truth?" she asked with a blend of admiration and horror.

"Only when it's convenient, and never to toxic dump sites like those two. The fancy word for what I do is 'disinformation'—that's what the intelligence services of the world call it. False stories concocted to cloud the truth and spread confusion. No worse than posing as a Vegas showgirl, or all that stuff you made up about the bills being marked."

"I didn't make that up," said Kittering. "All I said was it's Ricci money from a Ricci casino. That's true. She jumped in with both feet and told us everything else."

"Smooth," Dodd said with a thin smile. "Now listen, if they go for the idea, try to get to my Director as soon as you get back to Washington. I'm his fair-haired boy at the moment. See if you can get him to whip up interest in sending a Grenada-size mopping-up party down here. U.S. citizens in jeopardy, et cetera. Meaning me. I have a feeling our friend Dr. Pepper may be right about the Iran hostages and all that, but what the hell, it's worth a shot. If it works, great. If not, at least you'll be out of here alive and with nine working fingers. That's all I came here to do. Mission accomplished."

"What about you?"

"I'll keep winging it. Maybe I'll survive." He shrugged. "Just before I came down here, I had a little talk with my dad—"

"I thought you told me your father was dead."

"He is. This was a dream. In the dream, he was kind of an angel of death, he'd been sent to carry me off to the next world, but he gave me a few days to put my affairs in order." Dodd grinned. "That time is just about up."

"You don't believe in *dreams*, do you?"

"Maybe, maybe not. I've had some dream-hunches that paid off pretty good. He told me the next world is something like Nova Scotia. That was a cute touch."

"Dodd," she said, "what about the money?"

"Leave it in the p.o. box until this whole Vásquez thing is settled once and for all, until it's confirmed that either he's dead or I am. Because that's what it'll have to come down to, in the crunch. Until then, that p.o. box is the best place for it. There *is* a p.o. box?"

"Oh, yes."

"In your name?"

She smiled. "Of course not."

"You're learning."

"But the Señora—"

"Yeah, that part is going to get a little sticky for you. She could blow the lid off. If she's picked up, and they sweat her . . ."

"They don't have anything on her."

"When has that ever stopped them from picking up and sweating? She might get scared and make a trade, tell them about your p.o. box. Wham, bam, she's out and you're *in* the roach motel. So am I, if I ever get off Devil's Island here. Do us both a favor and, first chance you get, ice her."

"I-I'm not sure I can."

"Rosa would kill *you* as soon as look at you," Dodd said. "She's no better than her brother, remember that. She carries a razor the size of a meat cleaver in her purse and damn near sliced my onions with it last night."

"You two got that close, did you?"

"Reminds me," said Dodd. "Farnsworth. You won't need that key yet, so stay away from him. He's trouble."

"But cute," she insisted.

Dodd's echoing *"Cute!"* was a growl of disgust.

Across the room, Vásquez and his wife were finishing their own conversation. Rosa Maria was saying, "What about *her?"*—meaning Kittering.

"Never allow her out of your sight," said El Presidente. "If they have been lying, the first thing she will try to do will be to contact her superiors in the Justice Department, but she must not be allowed to contact anybody."

"Except Farnsie."

"Except, as you say, this Farnsie, if he exists . . ."

"If he exists," said Rosa Maria. "If the money exists. If the list exists. If, if, if."

". . . Then," Vásquez concluded, "you must follow her

83

to his apartment, break in upon them immediately, get the key yourself, and kill them both. Do you think you can do that, *alma de mi corazón?*"

Rosa Maria smiled sweetly at her husband and said, "What do you think?"

Part

12

"T HE Khyber Pass is neutral territory and therefore a good place for the three of us to meet," said the Director.

"Fine with me, sir," said the Chief, looking around at the popular Calvert Street restaurant. "I like Afghan cuisine."

"I don't," said the Director. "It's well known that I prefer the less exotic fare served at my club—which is why no one will expect to find me here."

"Afghan . . ." said the third man at their table. "I don't know. . . . Could have political implications, if I were seen here. Still, the fact that it's up here on the second floor is a nice touch. Not off the street. Covert."

"Our guest," the Director told the Chief, "if you don't already know, is from the CI—"

"Shhhh! Not so loud, please," said the third man.

"See Eye?" said the Chief, all innocence. "Do you train dogs for the blind?"

The nervous guest chuckled. "That's pretty good, Chief. Let's just say that I do." Squinting at the menu, he asked, "What's this aushak?"

"A kind of won ton," said the Chief.

"That sounds good. I think I'll have that."

"Not for me," said the Director. "I don't like Chinese food. Order for me, will you?"

The Chief ordered lamb kebab, rice pilav, and sautéed pumpkin for the Director and himself.

"Now then," asked the Director, "any word from Former Supervisory Special Agent Dodd?"

"No, sir," said the Chief, with some surprise. "I didn't expect any. Officially, he's a civilian and I don't even know he exists. Unofficially, I assume he has reached La—"

"No names, please," said Seeing Eye.

"—his destination and has his hands full without trying to find ways of getting word back to the Bureau."

"Of course," said the Director, with a nod. "We both have confidence in his ability, and I, for one, am certain that he will be able to extricate Field Investigator Kittering from bondage and return with her to Washington, safe and sound, without upsetting any apple carts."

"Apple carts, sir?"

"Diplomatic apple carts," said Seeing Eye.

"I'm afraid I don't follow," said the Chief.

"Our guest means," explained the Director , "that it's to be hoped that Dodd is able to complete his assignment without unduly offending this fellow . . . what's his name?"

Seeing Eye whispered, "Vásquez."

"What if Dodd does offend him?" said the Chief. "What does it matter? The man is a sewer rat. He deals in cocaine by the ton and chops off women's fingers and commits who knows how many other unspeakable horrors."

The Director said, "Calm down, Chief. Everything you say is true. But this sewer rat is also *kind* of a head of state. . . ."

"Head of—??!!"

"Not only that," said Seeing Eye, digging into his aushak, "but that little island is ripe for Communist takeover. A stepping stone to the southern tip of South America. It's got an airport, electricity, the works. This aushak stuff isn't too bad. What's in it?"

"Leeks," said the Chief. "The meat sauce is made with mint and yogurt."

"Yogurt. Uh-oh. I'll be on the throne all night. Anyway, we wouldn't want your Dodd to weaken El Presidente's position there and leave the country vulnerable to the Soviets."

"When you're ready for dessert," said the Chief, "I recommend the elephant ears."

"Air Force One" took off from La Calavera International Airport, carrying Rosa Maria Vásquez and Field Investigator Kittering to Argentina, where they would transfer to a jetliner bound for Washington.

Their escorts to Argentina were the same two men who had conducted Dodd and his hat box to the Skull. Seated in back of the women, they chattered in nonstop Spanish, which they knew was incomprehensible to their First Lady. It was entirely comprehensible to Kittering, however, who found it more diverting than an inflight movie.

"Pablocito," said one to the other, "if you were offered your choice, which of these women would you prefer to take to your bed?"

"You ask hard questions!" the other responded with a snigger. "They are both beauties. Why choose between them? If we are dreaming, why not take them by turns, every other night?"

"Indecisive!" scoffed the first. "As for me, if I could have only one, I would choose the Señora. That Italian fire! Those eyes! And her yellow hair, it maddens me!"

"It is not from nature," said the second, "but from a bottle. I do not criticize the lady for using such arts—my own mother, bless her, dyes her hair—but I fear that the sight of the Señora in the nude—"

"*Ay!* What a picture! Breasts like ripe melons, a belly like—"

"Lovely, to be sure, but I would prefer to take the *yanqui* Señorita to bed."

"And do you believe that her red hair is a gift from God?"

"Friend, you and I will never know."

The short flight to the Argentine airport provided no further entertainment, and after landing, the two bodyguards escorted the women right up to the boarding gate of the jetliner.

"I'd buy some magazines," said Rosa Maria, "but they're all in Spanish. This is going to be a long haul."

"I wouldn't know," said Kittering. "The last time I made this trip, I was chloroformed."

"I wish someone would chloroform *me*," said Rosa Maria.

Pablocito assured her, "There is a complete supply of classic movies on board, Señora, several of them starring either Burt Lancaster or Burt Reynolds."

"Swell," she said.

"Also Clint Eastwood and Charles Bronson," added his counterpart.

"Whatever," said Rosa Maria.

"Have a good flight, ladies."

"So long, boys," said Rosa Maria.

With a provocative wink, Kittering said, *"Adiós, muchachos!"*

The two men smiled weakly at her and turned to each other with blank faces.

On board the Argentine jetliner, Kittering was surprised to see a long perspective of empty seats in all directions. "Are we the only passengers?" she wondered aloud.

"Of course," said Rosa Maria. "Izzy chartered it just for us."

"That must have cost a fortune."

"As Izzy would say, 'chicken's food.' Do you realize how many *tons* of coke he unloads every year in the States

90

alone? Do you know how much just a *pound* of that stuff brings in? Honey, he could buy this whole airline with what he made between breakfast and lunch."

"Speaking of lunch," said Kittering, "I'm starving."

"Lunch will be served," said the approaching stewardess, "shortly after departure. Please fasten your seat belts, ladies."

Takeoff was a smooth, uneventful roar, and the stewardess was soon asking them their choice of beverage. "We have some very nice white wine, Señora: Chablis, Sauterne . . ."

"Got any Corvo di Salaparuta?"

"I'm afraid not. Would you prefer a soft drink? Fresca, Dr. Pepper—"

"*Hell, no!* Vodka martini, straight up."

"Tomato juice, please," said Kittering.

After lunch, the motion picture screen was revealed. "What's the first picture?" Rosa Maria asked.

"I am not sure," replied the stewardess, "but I think it stars Harrison Ford. Or is it Mel Gibson?"

"Either one of them can park his shoes under my bed any time," said Rosa Maria.

In a moment the film started in the darkened aircraft. "Oh, dear," said Kittering. "It's a Mexican vampire movie."

"Relax," advised Rosa Maria. "We're lucky. The last time I made this flight with Izzy, he had nothing but opera films on board. I was ready for the Napoleon farm by the time we landed."

When Dodd and El Presidente had returned from La Calavera International Airport after wishing the women bon voyage, they talked business in the presidential study. Both men smoked long brown cigars.

Vásquez inquired of Dodd: "What can you contribute to my enterprise?"

"Well, that list, for one thing."

"Ah, but my wife will soon have that list. Why will I then need you?"

"Because," said Dodd, puffing on the cigar as the wheels spun furiously in his head, "that list is only part of the story. Key executives in Ricci's coast-to-coast drug network. It doesn't include the ones on the pad—everything from rookie cops to judges and mayors and a senator or two—the people that money is slotted for. The pad changes a little bit from month to month, prices go up and down, people are added or dropped. That part of things Sal left to me. And I *never* write anything down."

"Possibly the people of this pad are dispensable," Vásquez suggested. "Possibly *you* are dispensable."

"Everybody's dispensable, Presidente," Dodd reminded him. "Fifty or sixty years from now, you and I will be long gone. But cocaine will still be here."

"You are a philosopher, Mr. Dodd."

"No, I'm a businessman. So are you. And we both know that the cogs work best when they're all well lubricated with palm grease. Ricci's machine is running smoothly. Why throw a monkey wrench into it? Why rock the boat?"

"You are mixing your metaphors."

"I'd rather mix myself a Scotch and soda," said Dodd, strolling to the drinks table. "Anything for you?"

Vásquez thought about it. "Something Old World. Noble. An English ginger beer, please."

"Coming right up." As he handed the hissing glass of carbonation to Vásquez, Dodd said, "And don't forget how useful it'll be to have an FBI man and a Justice Department lady on *your* pad."

"Double agents."

"Exactly."

"The trouble with double agents," said Vásquez between sips of ginger beer, "is that, traditionally, one can never be sure which side they are really on. You, for example. Would you be working for me, spying on the Bureau? Or working for them, spying on me?"

"Presidente," said Dodd, "just ask yourself: who pays the higher wages, you or the Bureau?"

"I do, of course."

Dodd smiled and lifted his drink in a kind of toast. "Then there's your answer."

"You are a cynic," said Vásquez.

"If you say so." Dodd tried to blow a smoke ring, but it came out shaped more like a boomerang. "Do *you* ever do a few lines of coke yourself, Presidente?" he asked.

"Do I look like an imbecile? No, but I keep a little of it on hand for guests who may care to indulge, or business associates who wish to sample the product." Vásquez pointed to a small object on the Spanish altar, of porcelain, only an inch and a half high and of about the same diameter, covered with painted Oriental faces and writing.

"What is it, a pill box?" said Dodd, picking up the tiny antique and lifting off its little lid to see the tablespoon or so of snowy cocaine inside.

"An old Chinese inkwell," Vásquez replied. "The writing, I am told, is an erotic poem. Go ahead."

"No, thanks, I'll stay with the cigar. Havana, isn't it?"

"Naturally. Fidel and I are old friends."

"Are you a Communist, Presidente?"

"I am a realist, not a romantic. I like things to work. Capitalism works. Marxism, which is romantic, does not. This cigar is good," he added, looking at it, "but they were better under Battista."

"I heard a rumor once," said Dodd, "that Havana cigars are made by Cuban girls, who roll the tobacco leaves against their bare thighs . . ."

Vásquez smiled dreamily.

". . . And that's why the cigars have such a wonderful flavor."

"I am not prepared to confirm that," said Vásquez, "but I, for one, have always preferred to believe it." He blew a long white plume of smoke from his mouth and studied it. "In the cigar factories of the pre-Castro Cuba," he said, "the cigar rollers of the delectable thighs were entertained and edified by a *lector de tabaquería.* . . ."

"He read tobacco?" Dodd asked with a blink.

"No, he read aloud from the writings of Victor Hugo, Charles Dickens, and other great masters. A charming custom, was it not?"

"They don't do it anymore?"

"A *lector* is still employed," replied Vásquez, "but he reads only from the complete works of my friend Fidel."

"Maybe that's why the quality of the product declined."

"I have often thought so." Tearing his gaze away from his cigar, El Presidente said, "You are right when you say that cocaine will be here when we are gone. It has always been here. The natives of the northern Andes have been chewing coca leaves for centuries. Amerigo Vespucci saw them chewing it in Venezuela five hundred years ago, and without doubt they had been doing it for a millenium or more before that. Dr. Sigmund Freud considered it a beneficial stimulant. It used to be legal in most countries. But now it has become, how do you say it, a 'not-not'? . . ."

"A no-no."

"Precisely, a no-no. So legislators pass a law, and what was legal is illegal, what was good is bad, what was honest is dishonest and dishonorable. But all over the civilized world, Mr. Dodd—your country is no exception—the consumer base is broadening while business opportunities shrink. What your Bureau calls 'crime' is therefore beginning to cut across class lines and merge with 'legitimate' activity, so called. He who was yesterday a businessman—and is today, by an act of legislation, a criminal—tomorrow may be . . . what? A businessman

94

again, perhaps?" Vásquez cocked an interrogatory eyebrow at Dodd.

"Could be," Dodd said, "but let's hope for the best, Presidente. If nose candy ever goes legal again, the price will drop to about two bits an ounce."

Vásquez shuddered. "Do not say such things," he whispered, "even in jest."

An eternity of hours later, a chartered Argentine jetliner thundered and howled to a perfect landing at Dulles International Airport in Virginia.

Its only two passengers emerged, their skirts wrinkled, their bodies and minds assaulted by the cruel and unusual punishment of pressurized atmosphere, of sitting, of frozen meals, of boredom, of half sleep, and of inflight films, which had included two Mexican vampire movies, one Japanese Godzilla movie, three martial arts movies of unidentifiable Asian origin—all without English subtitles—and no movies starring Burt Reynolds, Burt Lancaster, Clint Eastwood, Charles Bronson, Harrison Ford, or Mel Gibson.

In addition to these hardships, the nerves of each woman had been tightened to the snapping point by the necessity of killing her fellow passenger at the earliest convenient moment.

13

"I DON'T know this area," Rosa Maria said as they boarded a cab for the twenty-five-mile drive into Washington. "What's a really good hotel?"

"We don't want a really good hotel," Kittering replied as the taxi moved out of Dulles.

"What do we want, a flea ranch?"

"We want a middle-range place, off the beaten track, where we can blend in." She mentioned a name to the driver.

"What's first on our agenda?" Rosa Maria asked.

But Kittering touched a finger to her lips and indicated the cabbie.

Because the hour was late and the traffic thin, their twenty-five-mile trip to the hotel seemed relatively short. As they walked through its doors, Kittering said, "I suggest you register under a false name, Rosa Maria. See you in the morning."

Rosa Maria grabbed her arm. "Hold on. We *both* register under phony names. And what's this see-you-in-the-morning crap? We get one room, so we can keep an eye on each other. Hell, that's the whole idea!"

"Oh, is that the whole idea? Anything you say, Señora."

False registration accomplished, they rode the elevator up to their fourth-floor room, tipped the bellhop, and locked the door when he left.

Vásquez gallantly had provided Kittering with a full

suitcase for the trip, but she was too tired to unpack it, except for the usual bathroom necessities and a nightgown. Reflecting El Presidente's conservative tastes, it came to well below the knee, was black with red trim, and was hardly transparent at all.

Rosa Maria didn't bother to unpack either. "Man," she said, "what I could do with a hot shower."

"Go ahead," said Kittering.

"And leave you here to maybe phone your pals at the Justice Department? Not a chance, sweetie. The two of us take a shower *together*."

"The hell we do!"

"Or we stay dirty together. And don't get any wrong ideas about me—I'm no lez."

"The thought never entered my mind," said Kittering. She added, with a sigh, "All right, I guess you've got a point. Let's hit the showers."

The two women found the hotel shower stall a narrow squeeze, but the water was hot, the soap was sudsy and fragrant, and their jet-weary bodies felt as if reborn in the steam.

"Wow, that's an improvement," said Rosa Maria, wrapping her wet body in an enormous towel.

"I feel almost human again," Kittering announced, enveloping her pink self in another towel.

Rosa Maria collapsed upon one of the twin beds, sighing, "Christ, I'm beat." Then, without warning, she buried her face in her hands and began to sob uncontrollably.

Kittering was taken completely by surprise. "What is it?" she asked.

Rosa Maria said nothing. She continued to weep.

"What's wrong?" Kittering sat next to her on the bed and placed her hands on her shoulders.

Finally, drying her eyes on the towel, Rosa Maria said,

"My brother. I just had to have a good cry about him. It hit me all of a sudden."

Kittering nodded sympathetically.

"Sorry to be such a baby."

"No, no, you're entitled. He was your brother. You loved him. And then, seeing him . . . that way . . ."

"I'm okay now," Rosa Maria said after a moment.

"You'll be fine."

Rosa Maria nodded, sniffling, wiping her nose on the back of her hand. "Yeah, I loved him. He was my big brother, but he was so much older that he was like my father, too, you know? Our papa seemed like a grandfather to me, and then he died when I was so little. I hardly remember him. I was like a daughter to Sal, not just a sister."

"I understand," said Kittering.

Tears began to collect in Rosa Maria's eyes again. "So—so why did he sell me down the river?"

"Down the river?"

"Marry me off to that glass-eyed greaser and send me down to the ass-end of the earth? 'It'll be good for you, baby,' he said, 'you're getting too dependent on me.' Bullshit! It was a business arrangement! It was the only time I ever hated Sal."

"I think your brother loved you," said Kittering, "and did what he thought was best for you. I also think a few hours real sleep would do us both a world of good."

"Sleep!" snapped Rosa Maria. "Do I look like my head comes to a point? I'm not going to drop my guard for a second. *Sleep?* And let you put something over on me? Forget it."

"Rosa Maria, we can't stay awake the whole time we're here here in Washington!"

"Sure we can, if we finish our business and get out right away."

"How can we do that?" Kittering demanded. "First, I have to get that key from Farnsie's apartment. . . ."

Rosa Maria picked up the phone. "Then call him."

"Now? It's the middle of the night!"

"Quit stalling, copper!"

Kittering took the phone from her, and hesitated. She cradled it again. "No," she said. "I'm getting some sleep first—even if you're not." Dropping the towel, she slipped into the nightgown and climbed into her bed. "I trust *you*," she said.

"Big deal!" said Rosa Maria. "What can *I* do? Call the Feds and blow the whistle on you? What good would that do me? I can't go get that key myself because I don't know who or where Farnsie is."

Kittering yawned. With a wry grin she said, "Well, you might go berserk and slit my throat while I'm asleep—with that razor you pack in your purse."

Rosa Maria laughed harshly. "Did Dodd tell you about that?"

"He also told me you almost sliced off his prize tulip bulbs with it."

Rosa Maria laughed again. "Maybe, but what would be the point of killing you now?"

The last word hung in the air like stale cigarette smoke.

Kittering echoed it softly: " 'Now?' "

"I just meant you're no use to me dead. And why get blood all over those clean sheets? . . ." Attempting to make a joke of it, she uttered a false and hollow chuckle.

"But you said '*now*,' " Kittering insisted. "Meaning, after we have that key, it will be all right to kill me, is that it?"

"No . . ."

"Of course that's it, Rosa Maria. It's written all over your face."

"Okay, *okay!*" Rosa Maria said fiercely. "It's true. That's what Izzy wants me to do, told me to do. Get the key and kill you and Farnsie. But do I need that kind of trouble?

Me with my clean record? Oh, I let him *believe* I would, because I wanted to get off that damn island, away from *him*, and I wanted that list."

"The list, but not Vásquez?"

"Who needs him? With that list, I've got enough smarts to take over Sal's end of the business. Hey, I'm *family*. And it's about time the Ricci *women* started to take a piece of the action for themselves."

Kittering shook her head. "You're measuring yourself for a pair of concrete Reeboks, Rosa Maria. Vásquez would never let you cross him and get away with it."

"Izzy wouldn't have me blown away. The damn fool *loves* me!"

"He loves opera, too, but remember how he took out that singer when he didn't stop singing fast enough. Besides, I've got bad news and bad news."

"Isn't that supposed to be *good* news and bad news?"

"There's a first time for everything, Rosa Maria. Bad News Number One. There is no list."

Rosa Maria sighed and shrugged. "It figures. That Dodd can really sling it. I don't suppose there's any money, either, huh?"

Kittering was keeping about one and a half chess moves ahead of Rosa Maria. A judicious amount of honesty had been working well up to a point, but answering an honest "yes" to her latest question could lead to endless complications. The time had come to pull a Dodd. Wing it. And sling it.

"Not a dime," she said. "That's Bad News Number Two."

"I didn't think so!" said Rosa Maria. "Sal never would have trusted Dodd with that kind of spinach. He never worked for my brother, did he?"

Back to honesty. Kittering shook her head. "Neither did I."

100

"I bet his mother isn't even Italian," muttered Rosa Maria.

"Whose mother?"

"Dodd's."

"I wouldn't know," said Kittering, although she did happen to know, in fact, that Dodd's mother was of Polish descent.

"Who killed Sal?" asked Rosa Maria.

Back to slinging it. "Mario Fontana."

"You mean Dodd told the truth about something?"

Kittering shrugged. "You know what they say. Even a stopped clock is right twice a day."

"Who killed Mario?"

"Your brother." More fertilizer-pitching.

"*What?* Dodd said *he* did!"

"Just trying to win approval. Sal and Mario fired at the same time, killing each other."

"Christ," said Rosa Maria, sitting down heavily, still in the bath towel. "But . . . if there wasn't any money . . ."

"Yes?"

"What were they fighting about?"

Oh, what a tangled web we weave. Kittering moaned silently. What could she say? And then it came to her, out of the blue: "You."

"*Me?!*"

"That's right. That's the way Special Agent Dodd reported it to the Bureau. He was there in the house that night, of course, but not to do business with your brother. To arrest him. And Fontana. It seems that Fontana made an obscene remark about you, and your brother demanded that he apologize. Fontana refused. The rest you know. Sorry, Rosa Maria."

Rosa Maria smiled faintly. "That's okay. So Sal died defending my honor, sort of. That's just like Sal. I'm glad you told me."

"I'm glad you asked."

"But there's no money?"

"No."

"No key, either?"

"No key, no p.o. box, no one named Farnsie."

Rosa Maria shook her head like a shaggy dog drying off. "Then would you mind telling me what the hell we're doing here?"

Kittering winked. "Rosa Maria, we are *off* La Calavera. That's mainly what we're doing here. Which is exactly what Dodd went down there to do: liberate a hostage. Me. And he managed a little dividend—he got you off, too."

"Who asked him?" Rosa Maria said defiantly.

"Come on. Don't tell me you're homesick for El Presidente and Skull Island?"

"I guess not. What the hell, I'm back in God's country and rid of that soda pop swilling turkey."

"That's the way to look at it. You're ahead of the game."

"I got to admit it. You're right," said Rosa Maria.

"Then you won't put out my lights?"

Rosa Maria appeared to weigh the question. "Not now."

Meanwhile, back at Honesty, "I won't put out your lights, either," said Kittering. "Even though Dodd suggested I do it first chance I get."

"He *did?* That *bastard!*" Rosa Maria clenched and unclenched her fists spasmodically in anger. Then she sighed, possibly with fatigue. "He's a pretty good lay, though."

"Oh, yes," said Kittering, "but I've had better. Come on, let's get a little sleep."

"You've got yourself a deal," said Rosa Maria, and climbed into the other bed. In a moment she said drowsily, "Thing is, though, if there's no list, no money, no Farnsie, what do we do tomorrow?"

But Kittering was no longer awake. And when tomorrow arrived, its first pale tendrils found Rosa Maria sitting upright in a chair, her eyes and mind gritty from lack of sleep. She had not relaxed her surveillance of the redhead all night long.

14

"YES, Farnsworth, what is it?" the Chief said wearily.

"You asked me to report to you, sir."

"I did? All right, then, don't hover, come all the way *in*. And close the door. Now then: I asked you to report about what?"

"Dodd's mother," said Farnsworth.

"What about Dodd's mother?"

"She did honeymoon in Fargo with Dodd's father, at the Powers Hotel."

"Of course she did," murmured the Chief, who was studying his globe of the world. "Thank you, Farnsworth. Anything else?"

"Well . . . possibly, sir."

"It has to get a lot more interesting than that before I give you my undivided attention," said the Chief.

"Yes, sir. You remember my suspicions about Dodd's safe deposit box and his oversize jacket . . ."

"Oh, yes, Farnsworth," said the Chief, "I remember those suspicions, and I remember how you took those suspicions *not* to me, not to the Bureau at all, but to that lady investigator at Justice, because you didn't trust us, you thought we'd cover up for Dodd if he was found with his hand in the macaroon jar. I also remember—with a clarity like the finest Waterford crystal—that your suspicions turned out to be totally unfounded and we all ended up with egg on our faces. Yes, I remember all that, and I hope *you* remember that Dodd is now Supervisory Special Agent Dodd, while you are still only Special Agent Farnsworth, Farnsworth."

"Sir," said Special Agent Farnsworth, "Dodd is missing."

"Farnsworth—"

"Not in his office, not at his apartment."

"Farnsworth—"

"Not only that, but Field Investigator Kittering—the, uh, Justice Department lady you just mentioned, sir—is missing also. Not in her office, not at her apartment."

"Farnsworth—"

"I think there's something fishy, sir. I think they were in it together from the beginning and they've run off with the money."

"What money?" muttered the Chief, playing with his globe.

"The money Dodd ripped off from Ricci."

The Chief turned from his globe and said quietly, "You are very young, my boy. I suppose the year nineteen hundred and twenty-four holds no special meaning for you?"

"Nineteen twenty-four? No, sir, I don't think so."

"And yet it was a significant year," said the Chief. "For one thing, the American Indians were granted U.S. citizenship. The writers Joseph Conrad, Franz Kafka, Anatole France, and Marie Corelli all died. The composers Puccini, Busoni, Fauré, and Victor Herbert also died, as did the great actress Eleanora Duse, the architect Louis Sullivan, the labor leader Samuel Gompers, and the political leaders Woodrow Wilson and Lenin. There were some notable births, too: among them Rocco Marchegiano and Truman Streckfus Persons, whose names were later changed to Rocky Marciano and Truman Capote—perhaps you've heard of them?"

Farnsworth nodded.

"In England in that year," the Chief went on, "Edmund Gosse was knighted. In Germany, Marlene Dietrich married a young assistant film director named, if memory serves, Rudolf Sieber. Greece finally converted to the Gregorian calendar . . ."

"Sir—"

"Patience, Farnsworth, patience." Relentlessly, the older man added, "Iodine was first added to salt in that eventful year, to prevent goiter. George Gershwin's *Rhapsody in Blue* was first performed, with the composer at the piano and Paul Whiteman leading the band. Thomas Ince, the silent film director, died under mysterious circumstances on board William Randolph Hearst's yacht. Some say that Louella Parsons, who was also on board, knew the details of those circumstances and was rewarded for keeping her mouth shut by being given a lifelong sinecure as a columnist for the Hearst newspapers."

"Louella *who*, sir?" asked Farnsworth.

Supressing a sigh, the Chief droned on: "The Broadway hits of that season were *What Price Glory?*, *The Green Hat*, *Beggar on Horseback*, *They Knew What They Wanted*—it won a Pulitzer Prize—and the musical shows *Lady Be Good*, *Rose Marie*, and *The Student Prince*. Douglas Fairbanks—that's Senior—starred in the motion picture *The Thief of Bagdad*, silent version. Important books published in that year were E. M. Forster's *A Passage to India*, Thomas Mann's *The Magic Mountain*, and, thirty-three years after the author's death, *Billy Budd*, by Herman Melville. William Faulkner's first book was also published in that year, a cycle of poems, *The Marble Faun*. But the big bestseller was, as usual, a featherweight, *Jeeves*, by P. G. Wodehouse. Am I boring you?"

"No, sir."

"I'm so glad. We come now, Farnsworth, to certain events more closely associated with our work, law enforcement. In that same year, nineteen twenty-four, heroin was outlawed even for medical treatment in the United States, Loeb and Leopold were sentenced to life imprisonment for the murder of Bobby Franks, J. Edgar Hoover was appointed Director of the Bureau of Investigation—the word 'Federal' was added later—*and*—" The Chief paused for dramatic effect. "And, Farnsworth, *I* was born."

"Really, sir?"

"Really. Which means that I am *easily* old enough to be your father. So, my dear fellow, when you speak to me of certain alleged 'money' that you claim was 'ripped off from Ricci' by Dodd, will you not take it in good part when I tell you that this money is merely a figment of your perfervid imagination?"

"But, sir, Dodd is—"

"Dodd is on special assignment."

"He is?"

"Yes."

"May I ask . . ."

"No, you may not. Information about his assignment is to be given out strictly on a need-to-know basis, and you have *no* need to know."

"Sir, what about Field Investigator Kittering?"

"I can only assume that the Department of Justice has sent *her* on special assignment, too. Or possibly she's on vacation. But that's not any of my business. It's not any of your business either."

"No, sir, not really, but in a way, it is. If Field Investigator Kittering is just on vacation, or even on special assignment, I think she would have told me she'd be gone for a while."

"Why on earth should she do that?" wondered the Chief.

"Because," said Farnsworth, "she and I have—that is, I *thought* we had—sort of an understanding. . . ."

The Chief looked at Farnsworth with enormous surprise. "Did you say 'an understanding'? What a quaint, old-fashioned turn of phrase from a man of your tender years. Do you mean to tell me, Farnsworth, that you and this Kittering lady have been Getting It On?"

"I'd hate to put it that way, sir. It's deeper than that. At least, I thought it was."

"Of course," the Chief said, soothingly. "Please accept my apologies. Well, well, love's young dream, is it? In that case, my boy, I will be guilty of a wee breach of security and assure you that Field Investigator Kittering is not on vacation, nor did she abscond with any ill-gotten gains, real or imagined. I was informed by the Justice Department that she was called away, on urgent business, so quickly and unexpectedly, literally without notice, that she didn't even have time to pack a bag. Don't you think that's why she didn't get in touch with you?"

"Yes, sir," said Farnsworth. "Thanks for telling me. Uh, sir. . . ."

"Hmm?" The Chief had returned to his globe.

"Is her official business connected with Dodd's special assignment?"

"I suspect that what you really want to know is if they left town at the same time, in each other's company. The answer is no. Beware, my boy, of jealousy. It is the green-eyed monster, et cetera. I think that will be all for now, Farnsworth."

"Yes, sir." Farnsworth turned to leave.

The Chief said, "Oh, one moment. I have another assignment for you. It will involve a trip to North Dakota. Check out the Powers Hotel in Fargo, if it's still standing, and do a little asking around."

"Asking around?"

"Yes, see if any of the old-timers there remember Mr. and Mrs. Dodd when they were newlyweds."

"But, sir, that was *decades* ago!"

"Do your best, my boy, find out what you can. We must

be thorough. If the hotel is gone, you might nose around and find out when it was torn down, where the former staff are now, you know the sort of thing. Remember: you're the one who first suspected Dodd. So far he's come up smelling like an American Beauty, whereas you've landed in the chowder. Wouldn't it be a feather in your cap if you could prove that you were right all along?"

"Yes, sir."

"I suggest you just throw a change of socks and underwear into an attaché case and catch the next available flight. Best get a move on."

"Right, sir," said Farnsworth, heading for the door.

"Dobas," said the Chief.

"Sir?"

"Dobas, the Hungarian chef, creator of the delicious Dobas torte. He died in nineteen twenty-four, too."

"Sorry to hear that, sir," said Farnsworth, and was gone.

The Chief stopped toying with the globe and strolled back to his desk. Sitting far back in his chair with his hands behind his head, he conjured up fond memories of Fargo, where he had been stationed as an innocent youth in the Army, one unforgettable summer during World War II. He and his comrades had been billetted on the campus of the North Dakota Agricultural College and attended lectures in its commandeered classrooms—his first instruction in intelligence work, experience that was eventually to lead him, upon resuming civilian life, into the Bureau. The food served by the NDAC kitchen staff was better than Army chow, the dorms were better than barracks, and he liked the town. He didn't remember a Powers Hotel, didn't remember the names of any Fargo hotels, in fact, because he and his Jeannie, a teen-age waitress, had trysted not in sordid rooms, sneaking past leering night clerks, but among the trees and grasses just outside of town, under the stars. Ah, Jeannie, Jeannie, where are you now? the Chief wondered with a pang, and his eyes misted over.

He thought of Farnsworth and Kittering, in their own couplings. What did she see in the boy? he asked himself. He wasn't bad looking, the Chief supposed, in a bland, unexciting sort of way . . . clean-cut, perhaps a bit *too* clean-cut. Well, women were strange; the Chief had stopped trying to figure them out years ago when his second wife divorced him for what he considered inexplicable reasons. Perhaps there was more to Farnsworth than met the eye. Still waters? Hidden depths? This, he decided with terrible glee, required his personal investigation. . . .

He rose majestically from behind his desk and walked slowly out of his office. As he passed his secretary he said, "I'm taking an early lunch, Miss Moscow." It was an unusual name, particularly for an FBI secretary, and once, when the Chief had asked her if she would ever consider changing it, the middle-aged amanuensis told him that it had already been changed, from Moskowitz.

15

"I DON'T like it," grumbled Dodd.

"What do you not like?" Vásquez inquired.

Dodd treated El Presidente and himself to a pregnant pause, a dramatic stage-wait, building the suspense as he maneuvered his captor into the strategically desirable position. Then he said, "Those two women going back to the States on their own."

His statement of dissatisfaction was not entirely a scenario designed for El Presidente's benefit. By this time, he told himself, Kittering should have terminated Rosa Maria, but he knew she wouldn't have done it. No stomach for it. Oh, she was brave, she was tough, she was a top investigator, and in some ways she was as cold-blooded as he—look at the switch she had pulled on that safe deposit box!—but snuff a citizen who had no outstanding warrants? Never. He doubted if *he* would have had the stomach. He'd never iced a woman. And the only men he'd ever blasted had been slithery rattlers who'd slipped through the fingers of the law time and time again. Well, at least Kittering had been safely spirited away from Skull Island. Now it was *his* turn.

By this time, Vásquez hoped, the Señora had taken the opportunity to eliminate Kittering and the Farnsie man, to recover the key, open the post office box, and extract the contents. Was she capable of fulfilling the task? He was sure of it. She had the blood of the Riccis in her veins.

Would she return to La Calavera? Of that, he was no longer quite so sure.

Doubt had been gnawing at him ever since Air Force One had taken off for Argentina. He knew that she hated it here on the island and much preferred her native land. And it *was*, after all, *she* who had suggested that she be his courier to Washington. It had not been Dodd's idea, nor Miss Kittering's, and certainly not his own. He had wanted to go himself—but Rosa Maria had talked him out of it. And, of late, he had begun seriously to doubt that she loved him quite as much as he loved her.

"I confess," he said aloud, "that I never liked it very much, either. But the Señora persuaded me. Can you trust Miss Kittering totally?"

Dodd shrugged, looking up from the end of his billiard cue. The two men were having a casual game. "Can you trust your wife?"

"Of course!"

"She calls you a spic, you know."

Vásquez smiled. "Yes, an endearment of hers, because she admires my cleanliness. I bathe twice a day, you see."

"Huh?"

"Your American expression, 'spic and span.' It means very clean, spotless, immaculate, no?"

"Yeah," replied Dodd, squinting down his cue again. "But 'spic' all by itself is a term of contempt for anybody with Latin blood. Like 'nigger,' 'kike,' you know. Do you still think you can trust her up there?"

Vásquez looked at Dodd with dismay. "You are certain about this 'spic' word?"

"Absolutely. It's like calling you a 'greaser.' Six ball in the side pocket."

"Good shot," murmured Vásquez, his mind elsewhere. "I must follow her . . ." he said, more to himself than to Dodd.

"What? And leave me here?"

"You must come with me," Vásquez mused, putting down his billiard cue. "You cannot be trusted here. You would outwit these idiots who serve me and create mischief."

"Anything you say," Dodd responded with an inward smile.

"But who will remain in charge of the island?" El Presidente wondered.

Dodd suggested, "General Espinoza?"

"He has a brain the size of a garbanzo bean. But it cannot be helped. Yes, Espinoza. And we must leave soon. Today. Within the hour. If we do not . . ."

His planning was delayed by the entrance into the billiard room of Maestro Ottokar Schütz.

"*Mein Präsident,*" he said, with a click of his heels, "a vord mit you."

Vásquez nodded.

"Vot vould you say," Schütz proceeded, "in view of the fact that a Sicilian opera is no longer necessary as a friendly gesture to Salvatore Ricci, that ve drop *I Vespri Siciliani* from our plans and schedule in its place *Der Freischütz?*"

"My dear Ottokar," said Vásquez with a sigh, rubbing the bridge of his nose, "your contract with me expressly specifies 'No Wagner.'"

Stiffly, the Maestro replied, "*Der Freischütz* is Weber, not Wagner. And I confess that I do not understand this hostility to German culture."

"Maestro, I assure you—"

The artistic debate was interrupted by the entrance of the faithful Pablocito. "Presidente!" he said breathlessly. "An aircraft is heading toward the island!"

"Aircraft?" said Vásquez. "There is nothing scheduled."

"No, Señor. Unauthorized, unannounced. But obviously its destination is La Calavera International Airport."

"Have they been contacted by radio?"

113

"They do not respond."

"Has General Espinoza been alerted?"

Pablocito nodded. "He is on the way to the airport with a detachment of troops."

"*Donnerwetter!*" cried Schütz. "Is this an invasion?"

Dodd was asking himself the same question, and marveling at Uncle Sam's fast work. Possibly his thoughts showed in his face, because now Vásquez snapped at him:

"Is this some *yanqui* trickery of yours? Some plot you hatched with the Kittering woman?"

"Who, me?" said Dodd, wide-eyed. "I don't know what you're talking about, Presidente."

"We shall soon see! If they are U.S. troops, Espinoza will make short work of them . . ."

(I wouldn't bet on it, Dodd said silently, not if they're crack commandoes, trained in guerilla warfare.)

". . . and, besides," Vásquez continued, "we have *you* as a hostage. Pablo, seize him!"

Pablocito came stealthily at Dodd, saying, "Drop the pool cue, *por favor.*"

Dodd let the cue clatter to the parquet floor and said with a chuckle, "Presidente, come on. I thought we were partners. I thought we were pals."

"Pals?" repeated Vásquez, with a machete edge to his voice. "*Pals?* Dodd, you white-eyed gringo fishbelly, listen to me very closely. Merely because I share my Havana cigars with you, and my vintage Fresca, and my wife's— how do you say it— 'kitty'? . . ."

"'Pussy,'" said Pablocito.

"*Gracias,*" said Vásquez. "Merely because of these amenities, it does not follow that you and I are *pals.*"

"Hey, you've got it all wrong about me and the Señora . . . " Dodd started to say.

"Oh, *please,*" Vásquez cut in witheringly. "Do you think me a fool? Do you believe yourself to be the only one? Do you think I do not know that she has deceived me with

114

General Espinoza, with the tenor Montini, with the late Albericho, with almost everything in trousers except the maestro, and would have done so with him, too, except for the fact that he is—how do you say it—'goy'?"

Schütz drew himself to attention and proclaimed, with dignity, "It is true. Vy should I deny it? I am no Jew!"

"I think," Dodd said to Vásquez, "you mean 'gay.'"

"Thank you," said Vásquez. "But even though she has made me a *cabrón* with horns, I love the poor wayward girl, I forgive her, I . . . where was I?"

Dodd shrugged.

"Never mind. We will discuss our so-called 'partnership' later, when the matter of unscheduled aircraft has been resolved. You will come with me to the airport, under close guard, where the leader of the invasion forces—if such they be—will be able to see your gringo face clearly." Vásquez favored Dodd with an uncomforting smile. "It is too bad the Señora is not here. With her razor."

Prodded by Pablocito's gun, Dodd followed Vásquez out of the billiard room.

Maestro Schütz called after the departing men, "I am vun hundred percent Aryan!"

By the time the presidential limousine arrived at the landing strip, the unannounced aircraft had already landed. It was a small, propellor-driven plane, even smaller then El Presidente's Air Force One, and it had been painted a disarmingly cheerful shade of baby blue or sky blue, depending on one's taste in terms. Effective camouflage against the color of the sky, Dodd told himself. Also dangerous: in certain situations, it could be almost invisible.

The plane was surrounded by Espinoza's troops, all with rifles and automatic weapons at the ready. A gusty wind was billowing their tunics.

Espinoza himself, extravagant mustachios unfurled,

115

marched smartly up to Vásquez as El Presidente stepped out of the limousine. "Señor Presidente!" he barked, saluting.

"What is going on?" Vásquez demanded. "Who are they? Americans?"

"The plane is without markings . . ."

"I can see that!"

"But it appears to be civilian rather than military."

"Not a task force, then, in your estimation?"

"I do not think so, Presidente."

"Nevertheless, keep your troops on the alert," said Vásquez.

"Of course!" replied the General, saluting again.

"And, General. . . ."

"Presidente?"

"I do not propose to stand about on this windy airfield all day, awaiting our unauthorized visitors' pleasure."

"No, Presidente."

"Therefore, you will please have the goodness to pry open that tin of sardines by whatever means you feel necesary, so that we may sample the quality of the fish it contains."

"Yes, Presidente."

"*Now.*"

"Yes, Presidente!"

"Or I will have your testicles bronzed for billiard balls."

General Espinoza saluted a third time, executed an about-face, and marched briskly away.

Over his shoulder, Vásquez flung a question at Dodd: "What do you think? Your FBI friends? CIA? DEA?"

Dodd, in the limo's front seat, next to the driver, shook his head. "Not the Bureau," he said. "I don't think CIA. *Maybe* DEA." Dodd was trying to pierce the plane with his eyes. If this *was* Kittering's doing, who was in there? Green Berets? The Delta Force?

General Espinoza, bullhorn in hand, addressed a mes-

116

sage to the unseen passengers of the plane, commanding them to come out, one by one, unarmed, with their hands in the air. The message was given first in Spanish, then in broken English, then in fractured French, and finally in a tongue unidentifiable to either Dodd or Vásquez.

"What the hell was that?" Dodd asked.

"I think it was intended to be Portuguese," said Vásquez, "in the event, I suppose, that our visitors are Brazilian."

Now the door of the plane opened to reveal a short flight of stairs on its inner side. In a moment a man appeared, one hand hanging casually at his side, the other holding a cigarette. He walked down the stairs with insulting nonchalance, making no attempt to raise his hands. He was a man of perhaps sixty, his eyes narrow and unwavering, and he was dressed in an elegant sand-color suit of Italian cut. There was the hint of a sneer on his face, and more than a hint of insolence in his voice, as he greeted the welcoming committee with words as Italian as his suit:

"*Buon giorno*," he said chillingly.

Then, strolling closer to El Presidente, he added, "*Sono Raimondo Davioni, di Napoli. Dov' è Luigi?*"

"What did he say?" inquired Dodd.

Vásquez, who had gone pale, replied, "This man is from Naples, and wants to see the basso, Albericho. What shall I do?"

"Wing it," said Dodd.

"I've got to go to the john," Rosa Maria said in a threadbare voice.

"You know where it is," said Kittering. "And I'm *not* going in there with you while you sit on the potty. I draw the line at that."

"Who asked you? But I'm not letting you out of my

sight!" Her nerves screamed for sleep; her eyes felt like pickled cocktail onions.

"What's this all about, anyway?" Kittering asked her. "I thought we were going to trust each other. What if I do report to the Department? What's that to you? You're not on anybody's Ten Most Wanted list—are you?"

"You might make contact with Farnsie, get the key, rip off that list and that money."

"There *is* no list! There *is* no money! No key, no p.o. box, no Farnsie! I told you that!"

"So you say *now*. That's not what you said before! When were you lying, then or now? Don't bother to answer that! I've *really* got to go to the john."

"That's a problem I can't help you with."

"If I had a pair of handcuffs or some rope," said Rosa Maria, "I'd make sure you stayed put in that chair. But I don't. So—take off your clothes."

"What?"

"Do it!"

"Why??"

"I'm going to take your clothes into the john with me, dumbie. I don't think you'll go running off bare-ass."

Kittering stood her ground. "I will *not* take off my clothes! You're out of your mind from lack of sleep and behaving like a crazy woman!"

"Take them off or I'll cut them off, damn it!" shrieked Rosa Maria, whipping the razor from her purse like a scimitar. *"And maybe I'll cut off your tits, just for the hell of it!"*

Kittering slipped out of her dress, muttering, "You really go to extremes, Rosa Maria."

"Hand it to me. Okay, now everything else."

"Isn't this enough? I'm not going to walk through the hotel in my pantyhose and bra!"

"Off with them, hurry up, move it! Shoes, too."

Kittering divested herself of bra and pantyhose. She

118

handed these and her shoes to Rosa Maria, who said, "Now our suitcases—put them in the bathroom. Quick!"

The nude woman lifted the suitcases from the closet and placed them just inside the bathroom.

Holding the bundle of Kittering's clothes under one arm, Rosa Maria grabbed the phone with her free hand and carried it, on its long cord, into the bathroom with her. Kittering was left alone and totally naked.

She immediately lifted one of the pillows of her bed and extracted the nightgown Vásquez had provided her for the trip. Her upbringing, and long habit, had caused her to fold it neatly and place it there after arising. In some situations, she told herself, the long black garment might pass muster as a dress. Quickly, she pulled it over her head, slipped her feet into a pair of slippers that stood under the bed, and picked up her purse. Unfortunately, the purse had been relieved by El Presidente's security of the trusty little .380 Browning and mock-lipstick tear-gas dispenser that usually were her constant companions. As the toilet flushed in the bathroom, Kittering left the hotel room and ran down the corridor.

She took the stairs to the floor below, and from there boarded the DOWN elevator to the lobby. She walked quickly and purposefully through the lobby, with an imperious stride and straight-ahead glare that dared anyone to raise an eyebrow at her *outré* attire.

Exiting grandly from the hotel, she demanded a taxi of the doorman in commanding tones, and was soon being driven away by the biggest, blackest man she had ever seen. His hooded eyes had opened like fancy headlights at the sight of her when she had entered his cab.

"Where to, ma'am?" he asked, about a block from the hotel. A voice like a lion.

"Stop right here," she told him. "I have to make a phone call before we go on." She got out of the cab and fed coins into a pay phone, punching Farnsworth's apartment number. No answer. Then she called his number at the Bureau and was told he would not be in that day.

When she climbed back into the cab, a piercing blade of sunlight X-rayed her nightgown, confirming what the driver had only suspected till now: that she was wearing nothing under it. Washington call girls were getting bolder every day, he told himself. She gave him Farnsworth's address.

He nodded and hit the accelerator. "Ain't chawl cold?" he asked.

"I'm fine," she said, "but it amazes me that you can keep your eyes on the road and watch me in the mirror at the same time. How do you do that?"

"I gots double vision," he replied.

When the cab arrived at its destination, Kittering said, "Wait for me. I'll just be a couple of minutes." And she slipped into Farnsworth's apartment building.

A quickie, the cabbie told himself, shaking his massive black head in disapproval. As a valued member of one of the best Baptist church choirs in the locality, he was profoundly dismayed by his passenger's behavior.

Dodd had told her to leave the money in the p.o. box. But Dodd didn't know that she had other plans for it—had *always* had other plans for it, right from the start. Farnsworth had given her a key to his door. Using it now, she let herself in and walked straight to the bathroom. She ran her hand along the top of the metal frame above the shower door. She did it again, slowly and carefully.

A flicker of panic brought discomfort to her mind and body. The key was gone.

16

K ITTERING groaned. A sheen of sweat suddenly covered her from scalp to soles, despite the scantiness of her clothing. She ran her hand along the top of the shower door a third time, very slowly.

No key. Not even a shred of adhesive tape.

Farnsworth had found it—even though he never took showers. Found it and *then* what?

The Bureau, when she'd tried to phone him there, said he was not expected to be in all day. That was interesting. It sent the experienced Justice Department investigator to Farnsworth's medicine cabinet, where a glance confirmed the absence of his electric shaver, lotion, toothbrush, toothpaste, comb, brush.

She stalked angrily out of the bathroom and yanked open the door of his clothes closet. His suitcase—a plaid canvas thing she had noticed when she'd hung her dress there on an earlier visit—was gone. So were his clothes. All of them.

Skipped town. Ripped off the four hundred thousand from the p.o. box, probably, and flew the coop. Where to? Geneva? Swiss numbered account?

Damn! Kittering cursed herself for hiding the key in too obvious a place. And yet it had seemed so perfect, when he'd mentioned that he never used the shower, only the tub. Better than such "classic" spots as under the lid of the toilet tank or behind a picture on the wall. That would have been corny.

She jumped when the phone rang. It rang six times, seeming abnormally loud to her raw senses, before the caller gave up.

The phone call reminded her that Farnsworth might have other callers—in person. A cleaning woman, maybe, with a key. She left the apartment and the building quickly, grateful that there were no tenants in the halls or foyer to see her in the Kleenex-thin nightgown.

The cab was waiting. "Thanks," she said to the driver, who was telling himself that she must have racked up the *quickest* quickie in the record books. "Take me to—" Kittering was about to give him the address of her own apartment, but stopped.

"Yes'm?"

She needed clothes, but her place might have been staked out. Maybe Farnsworth hadn't skipped town. Maybe he had reported the key, the money. Maybe they were waiting for her.

Or: even if the Bureau and the Department weren't waiting for her, maybe Rosa Maria was. If her husband's goons could find her—and they had—so could she.

Kittering would have to avoid her apartment. A little shopping spree was in order. Thank God for credit cards. "Take me to Saks Fifth Avenue," she said.

"You got it, little lady," boomed the cabbie, and headed into the traffic.

During the drive she tried to rein her runaway thoughts as they whinnied and galloped out of control. Dodd had asked her to contact his Director. But that was out of the question now, if Farnsworth had blown the whistle on her. No Grenada-style rescue for Dodd, then. He'd have to save his own skin. Was there any way she could help him?

First, she had to help herself.

"Saks," said the driver, braking the cab.

122

She pressed a big bill into his big hand, saying, "That ought to cover it."

"It surely do," he agreed. "Don't chawl want me to wait?"

"No, thanks," she said. "I have to fly solo some time."

As she climbed out he said, "You be good now, missy, y'hear?"

She sailed into Saks, ignoring the stares at her garb. "Everything," she told an astonished saleswoman. "From the skin out. From the shoes up. And a place to put them on."

"Yes, ma'am. Cash or charge?"

An amazingly short time later, Kittering was striding out of Saks in a smart pants suit and walking shoes. She had left the nightgown and slippers behind, instructing the saleswoman to donate them to charity.

What next?

She needed time to think. She felt like sitting in a movie theater, half watching the screen, half ruminating, but here in Washington's downtown shopping section there wasn't a single movie house left, except for hard-core porn pits. No thanks.

She made an instant decision and sought out a pay phone. Punching out the FBI number, she used her crispest voice to tell the switchboard operator: "This is the Justice Department, and I have an urgent priority message for the Director from Supervisory Special Agent Dodd. I must speak to the Director *immediately.*"

"One moment, please."

She waited one moment. She waited two. All calls to the Director probably were traced and recorded as a matter of routine, she told herself, and this was undoubtedly a stalling tactic. She decided to fox them by hanging up and punching the number again.

"Federal Bureau of Investigation."

"We were cut off. I was speaking to the Director, and this is an urgent call from the Department of Justice—"

"Sorry. One moment. I'll connect you."

This time, miraculously, she reached the Director's secretary, succeeded in avoiding giving her name, and again said she had a message from Dodd.

"Shouldn't that be channeled through his Chief, rather than directly to the Director?" asked the secretary.

"Agent Dodd expressly said 'The Director.'"

"Well, why is the message being routed through the Justice Department, anyway?"

"I'm working very closely with Agent Dodd on this operation."

"What did you say your name is?"

"I really *must* speak to the Director right away."

"He's at lunch. I'll take the message."

"I have to speak to him personally. Where is he lunching?"

"I'm afraid I can't tell you that."

"He's at his club, right? I'll have him paged there."

"Lots of luck." The secretary laughed. "He's at Two—"

"Yes? Go on."

"Never mind."

"Oh, all right," said Kittering. "I'll call back. Lots of luck to you, too. Job hunting."

Kittering hung up. The secretary had said "Two—" before catching herself. That had to mean that the Director was lunching either at 209½, the posh Capitol Hill eatery named for its address, 209½ Pennsylvania Avenue, S.E., and specializing in nouvelle French-American cuisine; or at the equally posh 219, which featured jambalaya, gumbo, and other Creole dishes. But the latter was situated at 219 King Street in Alexandria, Virginia, and while that could hardly be considered far away, it seemed unlikely to Kittering that the Director would take the time to lunch there. Consulting the telephone directory, she looked up the number of 209½ and punched it.

When the restaurant answered, she said, "This is the Federal Bureau of Investigation. I believe our Director is lunching there today. I'm his secretary. May I speak to him, please? It's a matter of great urgency."

"Just a moment."

While she waited, Kittering tried to structure her message in her mind. Brief and to the point was best. Make it effective. Something that would achieve the desired result, do Dodd the most good. If only that key hadn't been missing! If only she knew what Farnsworth was up to. Was the Bureau suspicious of her, or what? It could make a big difference in what she would say . . .

A smooth male voice came on the line. "Yes?"

"Mr. Director?"

"Yes. Who is this? You're not my secretary."

"No, sir, but please listen very carefully. I have an important message from—"

Click.

Kittering stared with disbelief at the dead phone in her hand. Had he actually hung up on her? Just like *that?*

Then she saw the red-nailed finger on the phone hook, breaking the connection. Turning around, she said, "Hello, Rosa Maria. You ready for lunch? I could eat a rhinoceros."

The Chief had taken his own early lunch in Lafayette Park, where he had purchased a hot dog from a vendor and ate it while sitting on a bench, with pigeons and gray squirrels as companions. Perhaps, he told himself while he chewed the humble fare, this bench was the very one on which Bernard Baruch, advisor to many Chief Executives, customarily had sat, making the park his informal office. Or had Mr. Baruch not used one specific bench? The Chief gazed at the White House across the way. It was a touristy thing to do, which was why he had never done it before, and he figured it was about time. There was an old Washington wheeze: "The squirrels are here in the park, but the nuts are across the street." Democrats trotted it out during Republican administrations, Republicans during Democrat administrations, and tour guides at all times, impartially.

After his al fresco lunch, the Chief had taken a cab to Farnsworth's apartment, safe in the knowledge that the agent was on his way to the airport and thence to Fargo. The Chief had not risen to his current high position in the Bureau without acquiring a number of useful skills, and one of these he used to persuade the lock of Farnsworth's door to yield to him.

Once inside, he had not hurried his perusal of the lad's bachelor living quarters. The place seemed to hold few surprises. The limited record collection displayed what appeared to be the standard popular music of Farnsworth's generation—nothing to raise an eyebrow. A miniature bookcase the size of a spice rack held the past half year's Books of the Month. A coffee table, positioned just right for shin-barking, supported one copy each of *Time*, *TV Guide*, the *Washingtonian*, and that morning's *Washington Post*. In the bedroom, in a dresser drawer, a small hidden cache of soft-core pornography was so rigorously free of fetishes, perversions, obsessions, deviations, explicit copulation, or even good plain full frontal nudity that the Chief was disgusted at Farnsworth's lack of imagination. His own taste in such matters ran to high heels and garter belts, with or without long net stockings, but he supposed that sort of thing was gone the way of Gold Dust cleanser.

And in Farnsworth's refrigerator, there wasn't anything even as exotic as frozen tofu dessert. There were plenty of Swanson Hungry Man frozen dinners, though.

In the bathroom, after routine searches of the medicine

cabinet, the toilet tank, and other standard hiding places, he was on the point of leaving when, almost as an afterthought, he ran his fingers casually along the top of the bathroom door. Nothing there. On the point of leaving the room again, he remembered that there was another door in most bathrooms. With a mental shrug, he ran his fingers along the top metal frame of the shower door—and smiled a thin ugly smile, for he felt a small object taped up there. Carefully peeling off the tape, he held his discovery in the palm of his hand and silently gloated.

Well, well. A secret key. There *was* more to Farnsworth than met the eye. Hidden depths, indeed!

Pocketing the key, he had left the apartment just eight minutes before Kittering had entered it in her nightgown.

17

"WHO were you calling?" Rosa Maria demanded to know as she led Kittering by the elbow away from the pay phone. "Farnsie?" Her sleep-deprived brain seethed and bubbled with poisons like a volcano about to erupt.

"There *is* no Farnsie," Kittering insisted. "How many times do I have to tell you?"

"Then who were you calling?"

"I was trying to call the Justice Department."

"Izzy was *right!*" Rosa Maria cried with a jay-shriek. "He *said* you'd try to do that, first chance you got!"

"Why shouldn't I?" Kittering said. "I work there, remember? They think I'm still down on La Calavera, being separated from my fingers."

"So what did you tell them?"

"Nothing! Before I even had a chance to say hello, you cut us off."

"How the hell did you get out of that hotel? You didn't have one *stitch* of clothing!"

Kittering favored her with a rather superior smile. "How naive you are, Rosa Maria. This is Washington, D.C. It's a very sophisticated city. A naked lady walking through a hotel lobby is very much a what-else-is-new sort of thing."

"You mean you just . . ."

Kittering nodded. "Sailed right out the front door and got into a cab."

"But you were completely bare-ass!!!"

"Sunglasses," said Kittering. "I did have sunglasses on. And my purse. I carried the purse . . . down here, you know?"

"Jesus."

"What about lunch? I haven't even had breakfast."

"You think I have?"

"I know a great place called Two-hundred nine and a half. Expensive, but I've got a purse full of plastic. Used it to buy these clothes. All right?"

Rosa Maria shrugged.

Kittering called out: "Taxi!"

As the cab took them to 209½ Pennsylvania Avenue, Kittering wondered if Rosa Maria would have swallowed the naked lady story if she hadn't been punchy from lack of sleep. The FBI Director, lunching at 209½, presumably would not be punchy—he reputedly had a mind like the well-known steel trap. What could she say to him? Talking to him on the phone would have been one thing—she wouldn't have had to identify herself, just deliver Dodd's message and hang up—but facing him head on in the restaurant would be something else. Maybe she might . . .

"Hey," said Rosa Maria, "this taxi doesn't have a meter!"

"None of the Washington taxis do," Kittering told her. "They charge by a zone plan. But the cabs in Maryland and Virginia are metered."

Peering out the windows as they rode, Rosa Maria asked, "Do all the streets have letter names?"

"Going east from East Capitol Street, they do, from A to W. No X, Y, or Z. And no J."

"Why no J?"

"I don't know. There's a legend that Benedict Arnold was an officer in J Company in the army, and that's why.

You ought to take one of those bus tours, Rosa Maria. The guide will fill you in on all that stuff."

Rosa Maria responded with a wordless scoffing sound, then added, "I had enough of that crap in school."

"Oh, you're a tough little ginger snap, all right," Kittering agreed. "I thought I was tough, too, when I first came here. Then I saw the Lincoln Memorial, just as the sun was setting. Went all to pieces."

Rosa Maria shrugged. "Lincoln," she said. "When I was a little kid, I used to think he was Jewish."

"Lincoln?"

"Well, his name was Abraham. And he always dressed in a black suit and black hat, like those Hasidic guys, right? And he had a beard. And he wore a shawl. I'm still not so sure he wasn't Jewish."

"Rosa Maria, you're something else."

The cab pulled up in front of 209½. As Kittering was paying, the driver said, "Now, Franklin D. Roosevelt *was* Jewish. Real name was Rosenfeld."

"How about that," said Kittering.

It was a simple enough matter for a Bureau man of long experience such as the Chief to ascertain that the key that had been taped to Farnsworth's shower door frame fit a box in the Georgetown branch of the United States Postal Service.

He took a cab to the smart suburb—likened by some to London's Chelsea—and got out at 1221 31st Street, admiring not for the first time the flavorsome old structure that served as the Georgetown post office. It had been built in 1858 as the original Custom House to serve what was then a bustling port.

The Chief entered the building and walked straight to the boxes. He peered at the numbers until he found the one that corresponded to the one on the key, inserted the key in the lock, and opened the box.

It was empty.

He closed and locked it again. No matter. He would drop by every day. Something would turn up. And when it did, it would tell him something about Farnsworth. Something trivial, perhaps. Something dull. Something sordidly personal, but entirely the fellow's own business. Or—possibly—something sinister, something threatening to the nation's security. Whatever it was, no matter how small or insignificant, it would tell him something about Farnsworth. And *anything* about Farnsworth would make Farnsworth more fascinating than he was now.

As he was about to leave the building, the Chief noticed a yawning postal clerk depositing envelopes and packets in many of the boxes, from the rear. He decided to wait until the sleepy-eyed fellow had finished. Then he sauntered back to the box in question, pulled the key out of his pocket, and opened it again.

This time he was rewarded by the sight of a fat padded envelope of the bookmailer type. With a barely suppressed chuckle of glee, he slid the package out and closed the p.o. box.

He left the former Custom House, examining the package with interest. BOOKS, it said. No return address. That was odd. And why have books sent to a post office box in Georgetown? Why not to his apartment? Were they mildly pornographic, like that tepid stuff he kept in his dresser drawer? Even so, this seemed needlessly cautious for an adult man, living alone.

But what fanned the Chief's suspicions from a spark to a roaring conflagration was the fact that the package was not addressed to Farnsworth by name. It was addressed to something called Utility Services Supply Registrar. Pure gobbledy-gook.

And a nose-thumbing joke for which the Chief would make Farnsworth pay dearly: U.S.S.R.

* * *

Kittering and Rosa Maria had lunched splendidly at 209½, but the Director of the Bureau had left the restaurant before they'd arrived, so there had been no confrontation with him.

The two women had spent the rest of the day together, bickering, shopping, quarreling, sightseeing, dining, and thoroughly wearing themselves out. Kittering was amazed that Rosa Maria hadn't collapsed from exhaustion.

As the day wound down to its end and they were standing at the Lincoln Memorial, Rosa Maria said, "Rabbi Kaufman."

"What?"

"Nice old guy in the old neighborhood when I was a real little kid. That's who he looks like."

"Ah," said Kittering. "Listen, Rosa, I'm not going back to that hotel. Not after walking through the lobby like that."

"I already checked out of that place," Rosa Maria informed her. "Parked our bags in a locker. Why don't we bunk at your place?"

Kittering continued to fear that her apartment was being watched. "I've got a better idea," she said. "Why don't we split up? There's no reason for us to keep an eye on each other anymore."

"I don't trust you! You might try to contact Farnsie."

"There is no Farnsie!"

"Then why did you sneak off like that? Why are you trying to split up now? What are you trying to hide? I'm sticking to you like Scotch Tape! I say we check in at the nearest motel for the night and start fighting again tomorrow."

Kittering was too tired to argue. "Are you going to sit up in a chair all night, watching me?" she asked.

"I *should!*" Rosa Maria declared. "But I think both of us are too beat to do anything but grab some Z's."

The next morning, after sleeping soundly through a

noisy motel night, the two women breakfasted at a nearby coffeeshop.

Kittering said, "Well, what now?"

"No more museums, no more monuments," said Rosa Maria. "How about a movie?"

"I—" Kittering's voice withered in her throat when she saw who was walking toward their table with a broad smile on his face.

"Nice surprise," he said. "You're back, huh? Me, too. What's the matter? You look funny. Don't you recognize me? Hey, come on! It's me, *Farnsie!*"

Part

IV

18

VÁSQUEZ and his Neapolitan visitor, Raimondo Davioni, stood facing each other on the wind-whipped wastes of La Calavera International Airport. Forcing a smile, El Presidente said, in fluent if somewhat operatic Italian, "You are welcome, dear sir. Come, step into the limousine. It is so windy out here."

"Where is Luigi?" Davioni repeated.

"All in good time, my friend. Come . . ."

They climbed into the automobile, which began to roll smoothly in the direction of the palace.

"This is my friend Mr. Dodd," said Vásquez, "an American. Do you speak English, Signor Davioni?" Davioni shook his head. "Ah, a pity. Dodd speaks no Italian, I believe. But we must do the best we can."

"I am here," Davioni said with a pronounced Neapolitan accent, "to look into the matter of our brother, Luigi Albericho, who is much loved in Naples."

"A charming fellow," said Vásquez, maintaining his forced smile, "and a great singer."

"It has come to the attention of the brotherhood," Davioni continued relentlessly, "that you have been telephoning to engage a replacement for him. Has there been a contract dispute? If there has—" Davioni's voice grew steely. "—the brotherhood will take his side in any . . . shall we say renegotiations?"

Still smiling, Vásquez said, "You speak of a brother-hood. Are you members of a Masonic order?"

Davioni shook his head. "The brotherhood is a Neapolitan tradition known as the Camorra."

Even Dodd understood that word. "Camorra? That's sort of the Mafia of Naples, isn't it?"

In English, Vásquez murmured, "I am afraid so. What can I tell him?"

Dodd thought fast. Would it serve his purpose to help Vásquez out of this particular jam? Or should he let this Camorra iceman skin him alive? He tossed a mental coin and watched it twirl in the thin air of chance. Heads I help El Presidente, tails I . . .

"Tell him the singer just left," said Dodd. "He's on his way back to Naples."

Vásquez repeated this lie to Davioni in Italian. The Camorra representative asked, *"Perché?"*

"Now he wants to know why," Vásquez told Dodd.

"He quarreled with Maestro Shits. The maestro cut out his cannellonis, or whatever you call them."

Vásquez spurted a stream of Italian in which the word *cabaletta* occurred often, as did the titles of various operas. Davioni's impassive face showed no reaction.

"Signor Albericho was justified in leaving!" Vásquez declared. "Contract or no contract! To cut such cabalettas is barbarism! It is like hacking the limbs from a classical statue!"

Davioni merely nodded.

"I did not attempt to dissuade him from leaving," Vásquez continued. "I did not try to hold him to the contract."

Davioni nodded again, apparently satisfied. But a hard look came into his eyes. "This stick-waver," he said with contempt, "this so-called maestro—I have a score to settle with *him*."

"Please," said Vásquez, "he knows no better, he cannot

help it, he is a German, he lacks all finer feeling. Why, only today he tried to persuade me to cancel an opera by Verdi and substitute one by Wagner!"

Davioni clucked his tongue.

"Is he buying it?" Dodd asked.

"Yes," replied Vásquez. "I think so."

"That's one you owe me."

"We will discuss who owes who later."

"God help you if this guy ever finds out what *really* happened to that singer."

"Be quiet."

"You'll end up as minestrone."

"Shut up, I said!"

"Okay, okay, but he doesn't spikka da English."

"*Che?*" Davioni inquired.

"It is nothing," said Vásquez in Italian. "My friend is merely commenting on the weather."

"So you better keep him away from Shits," Dodd went on. "If he starts to give the maestro a bad time, the maestro might let the cat out of the bag."

"True," said Vásquez.

"On the other hand," Dodd added, "it could be a great love match. This guy looks to me like he'd be happy doing lip service to the maestro's, uh, baton."

"I disagree," said Vásquez. "Please be quiet."

Dodd shrugged. But, watching Davioni in the rearview mirror, he had found out what he'd wanted to know. The Neapolitan's eyes had flashed with hellfire when Dodd had impugned his masculinity.

He knew how to spikka da English very well.

Vásquez was chattering in a state close to hysteria when he climbed out of his limousine, along with Davioni and Dodd, and entered the presidential palace.

"I think," he was babbling in Italian, "that we should replace *The Sicilian Vespers* with a Neapolitan opera—*The*

Jewels of the Madonna. A beautiful piece, too much neglected these days, do you not agree, signore? And the major baritone role of Rafaele is actually a leader of the Camorra!"

Davioni said nothing. Vásquez called for cocktails and hors d'oeuvres in his study. "A Havana cigar, signore?" Davioni declined. "Ah, yes," Vásquez rhapsodized, "I can hear it now! The music of that score is delightful. Those two lovely intermezzi . . . Rafaele's seductive serenade . . . the fiery 'Dance of the Camorristi'!"

Vásquez hummed a few bars of the fiery dance and attempted a few steps that, to Dodd, resembled an uneasy blend of Irish clog and Mexican hat dance. He began to wonder if El Presidente had been sampling his own cocaine. Davioni observed the exhibition with the detached, tolerant distaste displayed by well-bred ladies when they see dogs in the act of perpetuating their kind.

Dodd had helped himself to a cigar and now sat happily puffing, wondering what was going through the Camorra man's cool mind. The Neapolitan had heard and understood everything that had passed between Dodd and Vásquez in the limo. He knew that Vásquez had lied to him about Albericho. He had heard Dodd say "God help you if this guy ever finds out what *really* happened to that singer. You'll end up as minestrone."

Meanwhile, Vásquez, nervous but not afraid, was humming tunes from *The Jewels of the Madonna* and overseeing the serving of the food and drink.

Dodd was contemplating the combinations. Vásquez, blissful in his ignorance, thought Davioni knew no English and understood nothing of the furtive conversation in the limo. Davioni, however, did know English. What he did not know was that Dodd *knew* he knew English.

To Dodd, Vásquez said in English, "I have had a charming idea. I will ask the tenor Montini to sing the song 'Santa Lucia' for our guest."

140

"How come?"

"It is a Neapolitan song. A tribute to the city." Vásquez warbled ropily:

> "Oh, dolce Napoli!
> Suolo beato . . .

"What do you think?" he asked Dodd.

"Oh yeah, I think you'd better get Montini to sing it."

Vásquez smiled broadly at Davioni, who regarded him calmly and asked, "Is that a glass eye?"

"Why, yes," said Vásquez, still smiling, until he realized that Davioni had spoken in English. Then the smile slid off his face like a label off a wet bottle: crookedly, and by degrees, then down, down, until it was completely gone. "Yes," he repeated. "Glass."

"I thought so," Davioni said. "It is rather good. Would you like to have two?"

"T-two?"

"I can arrange it. Unless you would prefer to answer my original question—truthfully, this time. *Where is Luigi?*"

Vásquez gulped. "Luigi . . ." he began to say, and sat down shakily.

"As you can see," said Dodd, "Mr. Vásquez is still a little shaken up by what happened to Mr. Albericho. He had a lot of respect for him. I'm afraid it's my fault he told you a little fib—I knew he didn't want to upset you. He wanted to break the news to you gently. But the fact is, Mr. Davioni, your countryman is dead."

"*Dead?*"

Vásquez shot a glance of hatred at Dodd, and Dodd hastened to say, "Don't worry, Presidente, I'm sure Mr. Davioni will understand."

"Understand what?" snapped the man from Naples.

"At first," said Dodd, "we thought Albericho had been hitting the vino a little too hard, know what I mean?

He was staggering around, his speech was slurred, he just seemed to be bombed out of his mind. And when he complained of a pain in the pit of his stomach and a splitting headache, even when he started upchucking, that didn't surprise us—he just had a large economy size hangover, what else? Even when his eyes got so red and he squinted at bright light, we didn't think anything of it—I don't like bright lights when I'm hung over, either, who does?"

"Yes, yes, go on," Davioni said impatiently.

"Well, it got a little more serious when he developed what looked like the DTs—but even that fit the pattern, if he was a hard-core alcoholic. Still, that's when Mr. Vásquez called in his own personal physician. Right, Presidente?"

Vásquez nodded, dazed by Dodd's recital.

"Your friend had become stiff," Dodd continued. "Not 'stiff' as in 'drunk' but stiff as in *stiff*. Like a board. The doc called it 'rigor.'"

"*Rigor mortis?*" asked Davioni.

"No, he wasn't dead—yet. But his temperature started to rise. Went from a hundred and one to a hundred and three the first day, then in the next few days shot up to a hundred and four . . . a hundred and five . . . all the way up to a hundred and seven. I'm talking Fahrenheit. And *then*—" Dodd frowned at the tip of his cigar.

"Then?" Davioni asked, leaning forward.

"Then we noticed the *swellings*," Dodd said hollowly. "As big as a grapefruit, each one of them." Dodd clutched himself intimately. "Here in the groin," he said, "and in the armpits. Covered with little red dots. The pain must have been something fierce. The doc said it was lymph glands swelling up. He called the swellings buboes."

"Bu—" The Neapolitan paled. "Then our brother Luigi died of . . . bubonic plague?"

"I'm afraid so."

"*Mio Dio!*" croaked Davioni, crossing himself. "The Black Death!"

"Yep. The doc said that back in the fourteenth century it wiped out a quarter of the population of Europe—twenty-five million people."

"I know, I *know!*" groaned Davioni. "How did Luigi catch such a terrible disease?"

Dodd shrugged. "Probably from a flea."

Vásquez interjected: "This is the flea season on La Calavera." He delicately scratched himself. Dodd hoped he wouldn't overdo the performance.

"Where is he buried?" Davioni asked.

"Ah," said Vásquez.

"Burial was impossible, I'm afraid," said Dodd. "The medical examiner insisted that your friend be cremated."

"Cremated?" Davioni echoed. "Luigi was a Roman Catholic. The Church discourages cremation."

"But," said Vásquez, "does not expressly forbid it, I believe I am correct in saying? Signor Albericho, in his final hours, received last rites from Father Ruiz, my personal confessor, and a proper Catholic funeral after his death. Only when these sacred rituals were respectfully observed were his mortal remains consigned to the purifying flames of the crematorium."

"This is a great shock," said Davioni. "I will require testimonials—documentation of these events—to take back to Luigi's family."

"No problem," said Dodd. "I'm sure the medical examiner and Father Ruiz will be glad to sign all the papers you need. Isn't that right, Presidente?"

"Consider it done," said Vásquez quickly.

Davioni sighed. "I will have that drink now, if I may."

"To be sure, signore. I will serve it myself. We have some very fine Italian wines here. Valpolicella Allegrini?

Rubesco Lungarotti? Or perhaps you prefer a white wine—Lugana di Franco Visconti? . . ."

"A little Scotch whisky, please, on the rocks."

"Of course." Vásquez busied himself with the drinks and, tray in hand, handed Scotch to Davioni and Dodd, and took a Squirt for himself. Raising his glass, he said reverently, "To Luigi."

The other men repeated the toast and sipped their drinks. Davioni said, "I will take his ashes home with me, of course."

"What?" said Vásquez, choking on his Squirt.

"Luigi's ashes. I will return them to his beloved Naples."

"Naturally," Dodd said smoothly. "It's only right." He got up from his chair and walked to the Spanish altar, where he solemnly picked up the inch-and-a-half inkwell and carried it over to Davioni. "Here they are," he said quietly.

Davioni blinked at the minuscule porcelain antique. "*This?*" he said.

Dodd nodded. "A Chinese funerary urn."

Vásquez added, "The writing you see on it is a prayer for the departed."

Davioni lifted the half-dollar-size lid and blinked at the modicum of powder inside. "I expected . . . more, somehow."

Dodd said, "The decontamination process doesn't leave much."

"Decontamination process?"

"Health regulations," Dodd said darkly.

"What is Man," Vásquez observed, "but a pinch of dust, after all?"

"And now," said Dodd, "El Presidente and I have some urgent business to attend to. . . ."

"In the United States," added Vásquez, "which means we must fly to the mainland at once."

"To Argentina?" asked Davioni. "I, too, must return there to make my own airline connection. Permit me to be your pilot, using the plane I rented to fly to your island."

"Oh, we could not impose—" Vásquez started to say.

"Why not?" Dodd interjected, not wanting, for devious reasons of his own, to sever the Neapolitan connection too quickly. "We're all friends, aren't we?" Surreptitiously he nudged El Presidente.

"Friends, yes!" blurted Vásquez. "Three friends! We accept your kind invitation, signore."

19

"**D**o you smoke, Farnsworth?"

"No, sir."

"It's just as well. The air in these little rooms gets stuffy fast enough without smoke. I used to indulge, but I gave it up five years ago. Doctor's orders."

"Good for you, sir."

"Very good for me. I had a smoker's hack that sounded like Mount St. Helens erupting. Nothing of interest to report from Fargo?"

"Afraid not, sir."

The Chief sighed. "Ah, well. There has been an interesting development *here*, however, while you were gone."

"Here?"

"Yes."

"What is it, sir?"

"All in good time, my boy, all in good time."

Farnsworth crossed his legs. "Who are we waiting for, sir?"

"Waiting for?" the Chief repeated.

"Who are we going to interrogate, I mean."

"Oh, that's such a spiky word, don't you think? 'Interrogate.' I prefer to think of it as having a conversation. Something that could just as easily take place in my office, except for the distractions. The phone. The view outside the windows. My secretary sashaying in and out whenever it suits her officious fancy. No distractions in here."

"No, sir. Who will the conversation be with?"

The Chief lowered his voice. "It will be an intra-Bureau conversation," he said with a sly wink.

Farnsworth's eyes widened. "The conversation will be with one of . . . us? An agent?"

The Chief nodded.

"Anyone I know?"

The Chief nodded again. "Someone you know very well," he said, "and who appears to have abused our faith in him most shockingly."

"That's a shame, sir," said Farnsworth cheerily, as visions of Dodd danced in his head.

"Yes, it is," the Chief agreed. " 'He was a gentleman on whom I built an absolute trust.' Do you know that line, Farnsworth?"

"No, sir."

"It's Shakespeare. *Macbeth*. King Duncan says it of the traitor, Cawdor. He also says, 'There's no art to find the mind's construction in the face.' "

"That's true, sir."

The Chief nodded. "Treason is a terrible thing, Farnsworth."

"Yes, sir."

"Do you know why there's no J Street in this city?"

"I never noticed there wasn't a J Street, sir."

"Not very observant for a Bureau agent, are you? But forget about J. Let's talk about other letters of the alphabet. What do the letters U.S.S.R. mean to you?"

"Same thing they mean to everybody else, sir. Union of Soviet Socialist Republics. In other words, Russia."

"Anything else?"

Farnsworth thought for a moment. "I don't think so."

The Chief said, slowly and distinctly, "What about Utility Services Supply Registrar?"

"What?"

"I believe you heard me."

"Utility . . . I don't know what that means, sir."

"Really. *Really.*" The Chief reached under his chair and produced a thick package with cancelled postage stamps on it. "How strange," he said, "in view of the fact that *this*—" He threw the package on the table between them. "—was delivered to *your* post office box!"

"What? My—?"

"Look inside it."

"Sir—I—"

"I took the liberty of opening the package and examining its contents, in the interests of national security, but I replaced them, and now, Farnsworth, I would like *you* to examine them, too."

"Sir," said Farnsworth, "I don't *have* a post office box!"

"No, you don't," the Chief conceded. "Not under the name of Farnsworth. But under the stupid, meaningless, phony, and oh-aren't-we-so-awfully-clever name of Utility Services Supply Registrar, you do! Now, let's have a look at the contents of that package, shall we, Mr. Registrar? Go ahead—put your hand in there and slide them out on the table. They won't bite you."

"Sir . . ." Farnsworth said in a pathetic tone approaching a whimper.

"Do it, Farnsworth!"

Silently, and with literally trembling hands, Farnsworth removed the contents of the package marked BOOKS.

"Wh-what is this, sir?"

"What do you think it is, Farnsworth?"

"Well . . . obviously . . ."

"Books, do you think? The package is marked 'Books.' But I would hardly call this stuff 'books,' would you? Printed matter of a sort, but hardly books."

Farnsworth shook his head.

"Not being books in any of the usual senses, this would

constitute a violation of postal regulations, I should think, wouldn't you?"

Farnsworth nodded.

"But I'm not really concerned with minor postal infractions, Farnsworth," said the Chief. "There's something much more serious at stake here. Do you know what that is?"

"I . . . guess so, sir."

"That's right. The reputation of the Bureau. The image. The morale. The confidence of the public. We must not have any more . . . aberrations. Ideally, I would like to keep this between the two of us, if I can manage that. Perhaps I can't. Perhaps the Director will have to be involved. Perhaps others, too."

"Sir," blurted Farnsworth desperately, "may I say something?"

"Of course. I *want* you to say something. I'm *longing* for you to say something. I'm hoping that you will fill pages and pages of transcript. Speak, my boy."

"It's just this. There's been some terrible mistake. I don't have a post office box. Somebody is trying to frame me."

"Who? Me?"

"No, sir. Dodd."

"Still harping on Dodd, are you?" The Chief shook his head. "Isn't the shoe on the other foot, Farnsworth? Isn't it you who have been trying to frame Dodd, ever since you and he returned from Las Vegas? Trying to discredit him . . . throw suspicion on him?"

"No, sir."

"And I wonder why? Merely to divert attention away from your own criminal activities? Or was it because Dodd was beginning to suspect *you?* But do go on, Farnsworth. You wanted to say something. Let's hear you say something meaningful. Something that will benefit your country and yourself. Talk to me. Tell me the names of your contacts."

"Contacts?" croaked Farnsworth.

"Shall we begin with the person who mailed you this package? The person who is so shy that he puts no return address on his mail?"

"I don't *know*, sir!" Farnsworth wailed.

"If you help me, I may be able to help *you*."

"Help me how, sir?"

"That remains to be seen. You appear to be perspiring, Farnsworth."

"Yes, sir."

"Do you find it warm in here?"

"Yes, sir."

"I, on the other hand, am quite comfortable. Could it be *guilt* that's making you sweat, rather than heat? Guilt and *shame*? Guilt and shame and *fear*?"

"Yes and no, sir," Farnsworth replied hoarsely.

"What the hell kind of answer is that?" the Chief demanded to know.

"No, not guilt, sir. Because I'm not guilty. No, not shame, because I haven't done anything to be ashamed of. Yes, fear, because I'm afraid I'm being railroaded, sir."

The Chief's fist came down hard on the table with a reverberating *CRASH!!* "Are you seriously suggesting that *I* am railroading you?"

"Somebody is, sir."

"What a pitiable object you are," said the Chief, his lip curling with disgust. "Cringing and whining and sweating with fear. Cravenly trying to put the blame on others. It's no use. Stop the pretense. The jig, as they used to say, is up. *I know.*"

Farnsworth blinked. "You know what, sir?"

"I found *the key*."

"What key?"

"The key that damns you. The key that connects you, as by an umbilical cord, to the box to which that package of

150

so-called 'Books' was delivered. What can you hope to gain by this parody of innocence?"

Farnsworth slumped in his chair and said sullenly, "I think I should talk to a lawyer."

"Eventually, of course."

"I mean now."

The Chief chuckled. "At this point, my dear fellow, a shyster would be about as much use to you as a third nipple. He would counsel you to say nothing, which would not be in our country's best interests. He would cloud your mind with legal jargon and hopelessly confuse you."

"Pardon me, sir, but it's you who're confusing me."

"Am I?" The Chief nodded reflectively. "If so, I apologize. Confusion was not my purpose. I had hoped to achieve clarity. And so, let us commence to . . . clarify!"

He spread out all the contents of the package on the table and said, "What have we here, Farnsworth?"

Farnsworth, after a moment, said, "Blueprints?"

"Classified blueprints. Highly classified. Top secret. Blueprints for what?"

"I don't know."

"A town house, perhaps? A new model car?"

Farnsworth shook his head. "More like . . . some kind of . . . missile."

"That's right," said the Chief. "Unless I miss my guess, an intercontinental ballistic missile. Of very recent design, if this date we see here is an indication. All of which you know very well, of course. That leads me back to my earlier question: Who are your contacts? Who mailed these blueprints to you? Who are you supposed to pass them on to? Why is a Bureau agent being used as a middleman? Let me hear some *names*, Farnsworth! Names and answers!"

Farnsworth pushed his chair away from the table and stood up.

"Where do you think you're going?"

"The men's room."

"Sit down," said the Chief. "You're very young. Young men have bladders of steel and can hold their water for a long, long time . . ."

"*What* key?" Farnsworth was wailing for possibly the hundredth time. His clothes were wrinkled, his smooth jaws were covered by a dark shading of stubble.

"*This* key, damn you!" barked the Chief, pulling the p.o. box key out of his pocket and slamming it down on the table between them.

Farnsworth picked it up and studied it. "I've never seen it before, sir."

The Chief snarled and hissed like a menagerie of caged beasts.

"But I can tell you one thing about it."

"Can you, really?" the Chief said in a dangerously pleasant voice. "And what is that one thing, pray?"

"The number on it isn't the same as the number on that envelope."

Grabbing the key with one hand and the bookmailer with the other, the Chief compared the numbers, saw the possibility of an error in delivery, but said, "What if it isn't?"

"Well, sir," said Farnsworth, "just that, even if that *was* my key, which it isn't, and even if I *did* have a p.o. box, which I don't, that package of blueprints was never meant for me."

The Chief's chin had become even more stubbly than Farnsworth's, and felt as rough as Ry-Krisp to the touch. He rubbed it now pensively and asked, "How long have you been living in your current apartment?"

Although surprised by the question, Farnsworth answered, "About three months, sir, that's all."

"You do use the bathroom, I suppose?"

"Sure I do, sir. I'm human!"

"Of course you are, my boy. Basin, toilet, shower . . ."

"Not the shower, sir. I like the tub."

"You never use the shower?"

Farnsworth shook his head.

"I see," said the Chief. "Then a previous occupant . . . well, never mind, I'll put someone to work on that." Briskly the Chief wrapped things up. "Special Agent Farnsworth," he said, "do I correctly understand that this envelope of blueprints and this key are not yours?"

"That's what I've been trying to tell you, sir!"

"And you do not rent a post office box?"

"No, I *don't*, sir."

"That being the case, then the Bureau's confiscation of this key and these blueprints is no infringement of your Constitutional rights, do you agree?"

"I guess so. Yes, sir, I agree."

"And do you agree that you and I should do all we can to please our Director?"

"Yes, sir."

"Excellent," said the Chief. "This, with your approval, is what I propose to do: I propose to report to the Director that Special Agent Farnsworth, discovering in his apartment—we needn't say 'bathroom' at this point, need we?—in his apartment a post office box key obviously hidden there by a prior tenant of unknown identity, became suspicious, took the initiative, and opened the p.o. box himself, finding therein a *misdelivered* package, intended for another box, and containing—*horribile dictu!*—top-secret ICBM blueprints, which he immediately brought to my attention. Would you agree with my interpretation of this incident, Farnsworth? Who knows, you might even become a candidate for promotion."

"Sounds fine to me, sir."

"Thank you, my dear fellow. Most cooperative. That will be all. Sorry to have detained you."

Farnsworth stood up, straightening his tie, grateful to

be off the hook. "That's okay, sir," he said. "It's good to be back in Washington. I see that Field Investigator Kittering is back, too."

The Chief had been studying the key and the package, but now he looked up slowly at Farnsworth. "What was that?"

"Nothing important, sir. Just that I saw Field Investigator Kittering this morning, soon after I got back from Fargo. She certainly was acting *strangely*, though . . ."

"Sit down, my boy," said the Chief.

Signor Davioni's rented plane, with the dapper Neapolitan at the controls, sailed into the milky heart of a cloud and out again. "Argentina awaits!" he crowed. "Fasten your seat belts, my friends."

"What seat belts?" mumbled Dodd, looking in vain for one.

"Where did you learn to fly?" asked Vásquez.

"Private lessons," replied Davioni, "from Mussolini's son. Ah, Il Duce! *There* was a man!"

Dodd, still in Ricci's clothes, had again arrayed himself in the Mafia capo's dark glasses and Borsalino hat and had donned once more the gray wig, in order to match the photo in the Ricci passport he carried in his pocket.

"Your disguise," said Davioni. "It is no business of mine why you wear it, Mr. Dodd. You have your own good reasons, I am sure. But it somehow makes you look, not only older, but so . . . so . . ."

"So Italian?" Dodd suggested.

"Exactly!"

"Thanks. It's supposed to."

Somewhat later Davioni squinted and said, "Perhaps I should finally begin wearing spectacles, but from where I am sitting, I can see only straight ahead. If I bank the plane a little . . ." He did, to the right. ". . . Can someone look down and tell me if we are flying over the mainland yet?"

Vásquez obliged. "We are still over water."

"Thank you," said Davioni. "That presents us with a slight problem which the Almighty undoubtedly will solve—to His satisfaction, if not necessarily to ours. Such, at any rate, has been my experience. I am a great admirer of the Almighty's ingenuity, but not always of His taste."

"What's the problem?" Dodd asked.

"We appear," said Davioni, "to be completely out of fuel."

Vásquez, who had been observing weather conditions through the window, murmured, "Perhaps we can float to safety like a kite, signore," and added viperishly, "on the winds of the approaching cyclone."

Part

V

20

"WHAT'S aushak?"

"Sort of like ravioli," said Kittering.

"I'll give it a try, then," said Rosa Maria, "but it better be edible. I don't know why we had to come to an Arab place, anyway."

"Afghan."

"Whatever."

"We have to eat. I thought maybe Khyber Pass would be one place where we wouldn't run into Farnsie. He's Mr. Bland—strictly a Big Mac type. And, being up here on the second story, there's less chance of being spotted by anybody from my Department or the Bureau. That's what you want, isn't it—me to keep my distance from them?"

Rosa Maria nodded. "At least until I can think straight, figure out what my next move should be. As for Farnsie, I'd *love* to run into *him* again. I wish you could have seen your face when he walked into that coffeeshop. The second he said 'Farnsie,' the bottom fell out of your whole story, like the bottom of a wet grocery bag. Everything tumbled out and rolled all over the floor—apples, oranges, canned goods, the money that didn't exist, the key that didn't exist, the list that didn't exist. Because there was the famous Farnsie that didn't exist, big as life, grinning at you." Rosa Maria began to laugh. "But I almost have to hand it to you. Yelling at him like that at the top of your voice, grabbing my arm and yanking me out of there

159

before I hardly knew what was happening . . . that poor nerd must still be in shock!" Her laughter subsided, and her voice took on a hard edge. "But *I'm* not. And I want some answers from you, fuzzlady!"

Patiently Kittering said, "Once more into the breach. *A:* There is *no list.* Dodd made that up. *B:* There is, or was, a key to a p.o. box, but it's gone. It's not in Farnsie's shower anymore; I have to assume he found it. *C:* There *is* a package containing four hundred thousand dollars of your brother's illegally obtained money that I, as a Justice Department investigator, confiscated to prevent a susceptible agent of Federal law enforcement from personally appropriating for his own use. But who may have that package of money now, I don't know. Maybe Farnsie. Maybe not."

Rosa Maria, skepticism seared into her face as by a branding iron, said, "This 'susceptible' agent you were saving from himself—was it Dodd?"

"I work with a lot of Federal agents from a lot of Federal agencies, Rosa Maria. Not only the FBI. From my own Department, from ATF, from Drug Enforcement . . ."

"And Farnsie," said Rosa Maria, "who *is* he, exactly? What's his whole name? He's not a Fed, too, is he?"

"Does he look smart enough to be a Federal agent?" Kittering said with pity.

"Maybe not, but he's smart enough to find the Khyber Pass. Look, there he is, over at that table."

"Oh, my God."

"Who are those other three guys?"

"I don't know," said Kittering, but she knew very well that two of them were Dodd's Chief and the Bureau Director. The other man, squinting at the menu, was not familiar to her.

"What's this firnee?" asked Seeing Eye, pointing to his menu.

160

"That's an Afghan pudding," said the Chief, "very nice, but a dessert. I wouldn't recommend it as a main course."

"Chief," said the Director, "I think it will be simpler if you order for all of us."

"Certainly, sir." The Chief asked the waiter for four orders of beef kebab and sautéed eggplant, with baklava and coffee later.

"It seems," said the Director, "that we have interlocking reports to share. Perhaps we should begin with Special Agent Farnsworth's, which I understand concerns the hostage, Field Investigator Kittering."

"Yes, sir," said Farnsworth. He told them of seeing the field investigator and another woman in a coffeeshop, and attempting to greet her. "But she called me a pervert, sir, very loudly!"

"What?" said the Director.

"Shouted at me to zip up my fly or she'd call the police!"

"My boy," asked the Chief, "*was* your fly—"

"No, sir! Then she just ran out of there with the other woman. Everybody was looking at me. It was very embarrassing."

Seeing Eye said, *sotto voce*, "You weren't surprised to see her here in town?"

"Well, I knew she'd been out of the city somewhere on assignment, but—"

"If I may interject," said the Chief, "we've kept the abduction under our hats. Need-to-know and all that. Special Agent Farnsworth was told only that the young lady suddenly had been called away on urgent business."

"But if she's back in Washington," said Seeing Eye, "why hasn't she reported in to Justice?"

"And why," wondered the Director, "did she treat Agent Farnsworth that way?"

"Sirs?" ventured Farnsworth. The other three men all turned to him. "To give her the benefit of the doubt, I think it all has something to do with that other woman. I think Investigator Kittering is undercover—and I almost blew it for her."

"But how did she get away from La Calavera?" asked the Director.

"And if *she's* back," added the Chief, "why isn't Dodd?"

"God knows," said Seeing Eye. "But I'd give a nickel to know how that Kittering woman got away from the island."

"Why don't you ask her?" said Farnsworth. "There she is, right over there."

21

THE tiny blue plane twirled and fluttered like a gum wrapper on the cyclonic currents, completely out of fuel and out of control, its three passengers being hurled bruisingly from top to bottom, wall to wall.

"*Santa Lucia, prega per noi!*" Davioni fervently implored, hands raised in supplication. "Mussolini, tell me what to do!"

Vásquez cried, "He cannot help you! Put your hands back on the controls!"

Dodd, whenever his head hit the ceiling of the plane, uttered only oaths, epithets, imprecations, and miscellaneous words of four, five, seven, and twelve letters. Silently he wished he had a crash helmet.

Dice in a cup, the men continued to be rattled and battered by the mindless might of the wind. It went on for hours, it seemed, but actually its peak force lasted less than one full minute before it began to subside and grow quiet.

Truly quiet, because the plane's engines, deprived of fuel, were at rest.

"Now, my friends, we will find out how well I remember what Mussolini's son taught me about *gliding!*" With this announcement, Davioni dipped the plane's nose toward the earth and shouted, "*Andiamo!*"

"You will kill us!" screamed Vásquez.

"Christ!" yelled Dodd.

Davioni, misinterpreting Dodd's expletive as an invocation of the Deity, asked him, "Is there a God, Signor Dodd?"

"Let's hope not."

"Ah, but see how He saved us from the cyclone."

"We're not out of the woods yet, Mr. Davioni."

"Have faith!"

Then Dodd, Vásquez, and Davioni all screamed together in terror as the ground suddenly sprang up straight ahead of them, like a vast wall.

Davioni pulled back on the wheel until he was almost horizontal in the pilot's seat. The wall disappeared. They all expelled long sighs of heartfelt relief.

The wall shot up in front of them again, they screamed again, and it vanished.

Then the plane bumped and rolled and shook as if the cyclone had paid a return visit, until the screeching sounds of skidding wheels told them they had touched ground and were, in a manner of speaking, landing.

Amid another trio of screams, the tiny aircraft came to a jolting stop, somersaulted, and ended its flight bottomside up.

For a great many seconds all three men were silent. Each thought the other two were dead. Then one groaned, another coughed, and slowly they began to rise to their feet.

"Nice work, Mr. Davioni," Dodd said, weakly.

"Thank you," replied the Neapolitan. "Now let us get out of here, if we can find the door."

"It used to be *here*," said the dazed Vásquez. "Why is it up *there*?"

Dodd quickly scooped up the scattering of pens, keys, billfolds, passports, and other items that had fallen from their pockets, and distributed them to their owners. Then the three men clambered through the door and onto the ground, to discover that the plane had come to its upside-down rest in the midst of a field.

"How fortunate the fuel tank is empty," observed Davioni. "Otherwise we might have exploded. But I must apologize. This is not where I had originally intended to set us down."

"It's a lot better than Davey Jones's locker," said Dodd.

Vásquez gazed at the sky and breathed deeply. "The cyclone has purified the air, clarified the sky," he said. "See? The clouds are gone, the sky is brilliant, everything smells fresh. We think of the cyclone as power without purpose, Nature on a drunken rampage, eh? But in truth it cleanses the world."

"It damn near cleansed my insides while it was at it," Dodd grumbled.

Davioni pointed an imperious finger, saying, *"Ecco! There it is!"*

"There *what* is?" asked Dodd.

"The airport. Be of good cheer. It is only five miles, maybe six. I did not land so far from our destination, after all. Come, my friends, a brisk walk will do us good, and then we can all make our connections: you gentlemen to the United States, and I to my beloved Napoli."

As they walked, Davioni said, "Presidente, you sang the Neapolitan song 'Santa Lucia' so vigorously not long ago. Will you join me in singing it now, to ease our march?"

Vásquez and Davioni began to caterwaul in two-part harmony:

> *"Oh, dolce Napoli!*
> *Suolo beato . . ."*

Dodd was eloquently silent.

Supervisory Special Agent Farnsworth, promoted by an appreciative Bureau for his intercepting of top-secret blueprints before they fell into Soviet hands, had been entrusted with the task of masterminding the surveillance of Field Investigator Kittering's apartment. He had assigned agents to watch the place around the clock, in four six-hour shifts, and had installed a wiretap on her phone. No one had gone in or out; no calls had been made from the phone; not once had it so much as jingled. She was much too smart to approach the place.

Why, Farnsworth asked himself, was she avoiding the Justice Department? He could understand her avoiding him in the coffeeshop, if she were undercover—even if he could not approve of her embarrassing methods. And he was glad she had tried to contact him at the Bureau that day. That had made him feel a lot better. He knew she liked him. He'd been at lunch, and when he'd returned, his secretary had told him, "Your girlfriend called."

"My—"

"That's all she said. Tried to get her name and number, but she just said she'd be in touch later."

He had expected her to call his apartment, and he had stayed in all evening, eating a Hungry Man frozen dinner, waiting for the phone to ring, but the only calls he'd received had been a wrong number and somebody in his building talking about a parking problem.

Farnsworth shook his head as he sat in his yellow Honda across the street from Kittering's apartment. It was past one in the morning. He had taken the midnight to six A.M. shift, magnanimously shouldering the most onerous chore himself, rather than burden one of his men with it, and now he yawned uncontrollably. How complicated and confusing his life had become, he reflected, since he had returned from Las Vegas.

He had been terribly surprised to see Field Investigator Kittering in the Khyber Pass almost at the exact moment that the CIA man had been saying "I'd give a nickel to know how she got away from the island." It was his surprise that had made him blurt out, "Why don't you ask her? There she is, right over there."

"The blonde?"

"No, the redhead. On second thought, maybe you'd better not approach her. If she's undercover, that might endanger her and spoil an operation. The blond woman is the same one she was with before."

"Good point," Seeing Eye had agreed. "Besides, I don't want her yelling at me to zip up my pants."

"Who *is* that blond woman?" wondered the Chief. "Anybody recognize her?"

All the men shook their heads. The Director said, "Looks foreign."

The Chief said, "Looks dyed."

Seeing Eye suggested, "Why don't you have them tailed, Chief?"

"I will, if the Director approves?" The Director nodded. "Farnsworth," said the Chief, "use a pay phone and put a couple of men on it immediately."

"Yes, sir." But even before he could dial, Kittering and Rosa Maria had left the restaurant, leaving a rapidly cooling trail behind them.

Farnsworth yawned again, and when his face reassembled itself, he saw in the rearview mirror a man strolling up the sidewalk, in the direction of the car. Farnsworth concentrated on being inconspicuous. If he had been wearing a hat, he would have tilted it forward, over his eyes. The man walked past the car, then suddenly stopped, turned, and glared drillingly through the windshield.

"Good Lord, is that you, Supervisory Special Agent Farnsworth?"

"Yes, sir."

"Burning the candle at both ends, aren't you? Young rascal! But I'm a fine one to talk," the Chief added with a chuckle as he walked back toward Farnsworth's car. "I'm returning from a late social obligation."

"I'm on surveillance, sir."

"What?" the Chief snapped viciously. "Who's under surveillance—*me?*"

"Of course not, sir! Field Investigator Kittering's apartment."

"Ah, to be sure. But, my dear fellow, whatever possessed you to take the graveyard shift yourself?"

"Sir," said Farnsworth, "I believe I shouldn't ask any man to do something I'm not prepared to do myself."

"Nonsense! I always do. Always have. How do you think I became Chief? How do you think the Director became Director? You'll get nowhere doing menial duties. You should be home in bed where you belong. Leave this sort of drudgery to underlings and flunkeys. That's what they're for. Remember, you have been elevated to loftier things. Supervise, my boy, supervise!"

"Yes, sir," said Farnsworth, somewhat crestfallen.

"However, as long as you've begun this shift, I suppose you may as well finish it out."

"All right, sir."

"I don't suppose you've seen hide or hair of the Kittering person? Very nice hide and hair they are, too, as I recall."

"No, sir, I haven't seen her."

The Chief nodded thoughtfully. "Curious business."

"Yes, sir."

"Well, good night to you, Farnsworth."

"Good night, sir."

The Chief strolled down the street, out of sight. In a moment the sound of a starting engine in the near distance shattered the night silence and told Farnsworth that the Chief had reached his parked car safely.

He had been visiting the apartment of an Asian woman who called herself Nancy but whose birth name was

168

unquestionably something more exotic. She had served in Hong Kong bath houses, San Francisco go-go bars and massage parlors, Nevada chicken ranches, and other establishments of like ambience, working herself thus from East to West, then east again to Washington, by which time the coppery cocotte was no longer in the first bloom of youth but rather a trifle shopworn, yet still capable of arousing the male libido to rarefied heights. Three years before the night of Farnsworth's vigil, she had come to the attention of the Chief, who had required of her nothing more than the wearing of a garter belt, net stockings, and high-heeled shoes while he plumbed her dews and damps from the rear. Seeing that he provided the wearing apparel himself, paid her not ungenerously, and his needs were simple compared to some of the truly recondite demands that had been made on her in the course of her career in public service, she complied without a qualm and with a reasonably convincing show of enthusiasm, once a week.

Then one night she showed the Chief a selection of photos, taken by a hidden camera equipped with an ingenious timing device. The pictures were of Nancy and the Chief in the midst of their sportive antics. She offered to sell them to him in return for a sum of money. The Chief threw back his head and laughed.

"Much too expensive, my dear," he said. "Why, some of them aren't even in focus, and none of them show my best profile. But if I could have one or two of the better ones enlarged, I might like them as keepsakes, something to help kindle the embers in the chill years of my old age. But not at *these* prices. You can forget about blackmail, my girl. I'm not married, and I assure you that if you were to show these to my director, he would merely ask you for a date. If you think *I'm* bizarre . . . no, no, my child, you wouldn't like him at *all*. So, you see, these wretched tintypes are no threat to me. On the other hand, do you know the penalty in this country for attempting to extort money from a Federal law enforcement officer? No? *Death.*"

The ignorant woman had believed him. Weeping and wringing her hands, she had begged him not to report her crime. "My dear," the Chief had said, "I've grown quite fond of you, so I am inclined to show you mercy. If you will turn over your camera to me, and all the photos you have of other men so that I may destroy them, and solemnly swear to me that you will never do this sort of thing again, I will allow this to remain our little secret."

At first Nancy denied having other such photos, but after the Chief graphically described the crackling, sizzling tortures of the electric chair, she broke down and surrendered her entire file of photographs (which of course he did not destroy but kept, together with the names and addresses of the men, some of whom were prominent Washingtonians). "Very well," he had said to the abject Nancy that night three years before, "there is just one more thing. You will not leave town or change your local address without my permission. My agents will be watching you twenty-four hours a day, every day, forever—you won't see them, but they will see you—and if you disobey me, I will know it, and I will make sure that you are *burned alive in the electric chair*. Do you understand? Good. On your knees!"

The night and loneliness hung heavily on Farnsworth as he sat in his car: he could feel the weight of them, like thick capes. He thought about Kittering. Her eyes, her lips, her smooth bare shoulders, her . . .

No, no, he had to stop thinking about her that way. She was a person under surveillance, even under suspicion, perhaps. Certainly there were serious questions being raised about her by the Justice Department, the Bureau, the CIA. He couldn't let his emotions get the upper hand.

It was just his luck, he said to himself sourly. Just when

he'd found the girl of his dreams and was thinking of popping the question, she had to get herself abducted by some south-of-the-border dictator and then involved in . . . in *what?*

Why couldn't things ever be simple?

Still, he had to admit that, once in a while, he did luck out and come up smelling like a rose. That crazy business of the key and the post office box and the blueprints (what the dickens was *that* all about?) had landed him a promotion, thanks to the way the Chief had handled it.

The Chief was a strange man. Unconventional. Unethical, some might have said. But Farnsworth had no cause to complain.

The passenger door of his car opened suddenly and a woman was sitting beside him in the dark, almost before he realized it. "Drive," she said.

He turned to her with happy surprise, which changed to another kind of surprise when he realized that she was not red-headed Kittering but an unsmiling dark-eyed woman with the black straight bangs of an Oriental. In her hand—barely visible in the scant light, but visible enough to intimidate Farnsworth—was the frosty metallic glimmer of a deadly weapon.

22

"FEDERAL Bureau of Investigation."

"Let me talk to Farnsie."

"I'm sorry?"

"Farnsie, Farnsie, come on, you know who I mean. I've got to talk to him right away. Hook us up."

"One moment, please."

After several moments the voice of another woman had come on the line. "Supervisory Special Agent Farnsworth's office. Can I help you?"

"Is he there?"

"Who's calling, please?"

"This is his girlfriend. Can I talk to him?"

"He's not in. If you leave your name and number—"

"He *knows* my name and number, I'm his *girl!* That's okay, I'll be in touch later. See you around." She had hung up quickly, chuckling with satisfaction.

Now she knew his name, rank, and serial number, she told herself. More important, she knew where to find him: in that eyesore building in the Federal Triangle. Rosa Maria had smiled, planning her next move.

She had grown tired of hotel rooms and motel rooms. Tired of living with a woman. Tired of lies: Dodd's lies and Kittering's lies. She had never heard of Pirandello—and if she ever had, probably she would have thought he was the owner of an Italian restaurant—but that did not prevent her from feeling the eerie, uneasy *pirandellismo* of the situation. Reality was shifting and changing under her feet and in front of her eyes. Dodd said one thing, Kittering said another, then Kittering retracted her contradiction, claiming that *some* of Dodd's statements were true, some were not, until Rosa Maria's head was spinning. First there was four hundred thousand dollars, then there wasn't, now there was again, but it was lost. First there was a list, then there wasn't, now there *still* wasn't. First there was Farnsie, then there wasn't, and now there sure as hell was.

But *who* was Farnsie? she had wondered. Kittering hadn't told her. And what was his real name?

Kittering had said she hadn't recognized the other men with Farnsie at the Khyber Pass. Another lie? Who knew? To Rosa Maria's Mafia-bred nose, the men had smelled like heat. Probably Federal, this being Washington. And that could mean Farnsie was one of them. But what kind? CIA? FBI? DEA? ATF? The town had more fuzz than a loaf of month-old bread.

She had decided to find out.

And so, in a rare moment of relative privacy in a rest room, she had looked up the FBI's number in the telephone directory and dialed it from the ladies' room pay phone.

The rest was even easier.

She staked out the FBI Building, suitably disguised in sunglasses, camera, guide book to Washington, stout walking shoes, and a wig of straight, jet-black hair to hide her blinding canary-color tresses.

Many people entered and left the building during the course of the afternoon. She recognized the Chief as he strolled smartly out at closing time. A little later she spotted Farnsworth, and kept her eye on him as he hailed a passing cab on Pennsylvania Avenue.

Usually he walked to the nearby Metro station and rode the subway home, but that night he was eager to get back to his apartment as early as possible, in case his "girl-friend" called again. He had a strong yearning to talk to Kittering, and hoped she would indeed get in touch. When his secretary had told him his girl had called, he'd suffered through an inner struggle: Should he report the call to the Chief? He'd been torn in two directions by conflicting loyalties, but in the end, love had conquered all. He hadn't told the Chief.

Rosa Maria, in her wig and other paraphernalia, immediately hailed another in the stream of plentiful taxis, climbed in with camera swinging from her neck, and flashed her driver's license at the cabbie so briefly that he had no time to register it on his consciousness. "Federal agent," she said in clipped, authoritative tones, the FBI Building in the background lending weight to her voice. "Follow that cab."

"Okay," he said, and did as he was told, following Farnsworth's taxi east on Pennsylvania to 11th Street, then turning north.

After a few minutes the driver asked, "You really a Federal agent, lady?"

Rose Maria lifted the ebony wig for a moment to reveal a flash of her blond head. "Why do you think I'm wearing this? For trick-or-treat?"

When Farnsworth's cab pulled up to his apartment building, Rosa Maria instructed her driver to cruise past at a moderate speed. Through the rear window, she watched Farnsworth enter the building. "Okay, let me off here," she said, handing the cabbie a large tip.

"Wow, thanks. Hey, you know, Federal agents never used to have such great shapes. Want to go out with me some time?"

"You're sweet, but actually I'm a guy in drag. So long, buddy. Play safe."

She walked for a while, in her flat tourist shoes, found a spot where she could get a sandwich, and again made use of a phone directory. There were a few Farnsworths listed, and she didn't know her man's first name, but no problem: she did know his address now, and was able to pick him out quickly. She scribbled his telephone number on a paper napkin and, a little later, dialed it from a different phone to make sure he was still home.

"Hello?" he said with appealing, boyish eagerness. Rosa Maria recognized his voice from the coffeeshop incident.

"Herman?" she demanded in an eccentric register.

"No, ma'am," he replied with audible disappointment. "You have the wrong number."

"Sorry, mister."

Then she called Kittering, at the hotel where they were currently staying.

"Rosa Maria? Where have you *been?*"

"Oh, here and there. Shopping. Bought a camera, walking shoes, sunglasses. Tourist stuff, you know."

"I couldn't imagine what had happened to you," said Kittering.

"Nothing happened. Aren't you the one who said we ought to split up, there was no reason for us to keep an eye on each other anymore?"

"That's true, but—"

"So I agree with you. And I'm having myself a ball. Maybe I'll see you around, huh? Hang in there, sister."

Rosa Maria strolled past Farnsworth's building, enjoying a sense of newfound knowledge, newfound power. As is often the case, she wasn't quite sure what to do with her newfound power.

A car turned off the street into the building's underground parking facility, a wrought-iron gate tilting up to admit it. It was a classic Studebaker Lark convertible, black, top down, in mint condition, driven by a balding, middle-aged man. Rosa Maria thought about this for a moment. Did Farnsworth keep a car in there? she wondered. He had taken a taxi from the Triangle, but that didn't mean anything—lots of people left their cars at home for weekend use and got to work by other means, rather than buck traffic.

That would make things more difficult for her. Keeping an eye on the main entrance, on the lookout for a Farnsworth on foot, would be tough enough. Watching the parking facility, too, for a car she didn't know the make or model or color of—and at night, yet—would complicate matters.

She'd just have to find out if he kept a car there, and what kind of car it was. But how?

Ask him, that's how.

She had been meaning to phone him again anyway, to make sure he was still home, and this would be killing two birds with one stone. She sought out the nearest pay phone.

He answered quickly, on the first ring. "Hello?" Still eager, but edged with desperation.

"Mr. Farnsworth?"

"Yes."

"This is Mrs. Shzmmmmmmmmm on the mmmth floor. I can't back my car out because you got me wedged in so tight, sort of at an angle, know what I mean? You own that nice Studebaker convertible, don't you?"

"No, ma'am. That's Mr. Whittaker's car. Mine is the yellow Honda."

"Oh, I'm *so* sorry to have bothered you! I'll call Mr. Whittaker. Thank you."

"Quite all right."

When she hung up, sputtering with laughter, Rosa Maria's mind began to concoct elaborate schemes: hiding in the shadows until the next car turned in to park and the iron grillwork opened, then scampering into the underground parking facility, finding Farnsworth's car, wire-coat-hangering the door open (her brother had shown her how when she was just a kid), stretching out on the backseat until he came down and got into the car . . .

No, wait a minute. He might stay home all night. She could be *stuck* in there, with not even a bathroom. Forget it.

She would watch the building—until midnight. That would be enough. If he didn't show his face, or Kittering didn't show up to visit him, she'd go back to the hotel and start again bright and early in the A.M.

He did show his face. Behind the windshield of his yellow Honda, which rolled out from behind the iron gate at a quarter to twelve—just fifteen minutes before Rosa Maria would have thrown in the towel.

Luck was with her, for, although cabs were less available at that hour, one rolled by almost immediately. She whistled it down, scrambled in, and pulled the driver's license trick again, snapping, "Federal agent. See that yellow Honda? Don't lose it!"

"Yeah, yeah, okay. I *thought* it was you, mister, but I couldn't be sure in the dark. Boy, you guys sure work late."

"So do you, stud."

"You know, it's amazing what you do with your voice. I mean you really sound like a chick. How do you do that, hormone injections?"

"Surgery."

"On your voice box?"

"Lower down."

"Oh my God."

Farnsworth parked. Rosa Maria paid off her driver and kept an eye on the Honda from a safe distance.

Farnsworth got out and exchanged a few words with a man in another parked car. The other man drove away. Farnsworth returned to his Honda. Rosa Maria waited for an hour—and was about to make her move when a man walked past the Honda, stopped, and talked to Farnsworth as if he knew him. She couldn't be sure, but he looked like one of the men at the Khyber Pass, the man she had seen leaving the FBI Building earlier that day. He walked away, got into another car, and drove off.

She walked quickly to the Honda, jerked open the passenger door, and slid next to Farnsworth, saying, "Drive."

He turned to her with a smile that evaporated when he saw what she was holding at his crotch. "Hey, wha-what's that?" he stammered. "A razor?"

"It ain't chopsticks, Farnsie, and unless you want that sweeta sauseetch of yours to end up as pizza topping, you'd better do what Mamma says and *drive*."

23

"**D**RIVE *where?*"

"Just drive," commanded Rosa Maria, brandishing her razor. "I'll tell you where when I'm ready."

Farnsworth started up the Honda and pulled away from the curb. In the dark, and in the black wig of Oriental density, he did not recognize her as the woman he had seen with Kittering.

"Who are you, miss?"

"Never mind."

"You seem to know who I am. You called me 'Farnsie.' Only my close friends and associates call me that."

"So what?"

"Nothing. What do you want?"

"I want the money."

"You mean this is a stickup? All I've got on me is about twenty dollars and some small change . . ."

"Not that kind of money," Rosa Maria said in disgust. "I mean *the* money. The four hundred king-size."

"Huh?"

"Four hundred thousand clamburgers, you wimp!"

Farnsworth's lips went slack with awe. "I don't have that kind of money, miss," he said. "I don't even *dream* of that kind of money. I think you must be mistaking me for somebody else."

Rosa Maria snarled. "Aren't you Supervisory Special Agent Farnsworth of the FBI?"

He nodded.

"Then there's no mistake. Drive back to your place."

"What?"

"Your place, *your* place! What's the matter, you deaf or something? We can talk better in your apartment . . . unless there's someone else there?"

The razor at his groin discouraged lying. "No," he said. "Not a soul."

"Good. I've been on my feet all day. I want to relax . . . get out of these shoes . . . maybe take a shower . . ."

"Sure," he said. He would have said anything.

After he had parked the Honda under the building and they had taken the elevator up to his apartment, he asked her, "Have we ever met before?"

"What do you think?" she responded.

"Here in the light, you seem a little familiar, but . . . no, I guess not. You're a beautiful lady, and I'm sure I'd remember if we'd met before. I know I couldn't forget that lovely black hair."

"Flattery will get you everywhere," said Rosa Maria. "Do you still claim you don't know anything about any four hundred biggies?"

"You've got the wrong person, honest."

"How about a list?"

"A list of what?"

Rosa Maria sighed and yanked off her shoes. "Well, I'll say this for you, Farnsie. You *look* like you're telling the truth. Where's that shower?"

"In the bathroom, of course."

"I hope it's in good working order."

"I guess it is. I never use it."

"Uh-huh."

"I mean, I prefer the tub."

180

"Yeah, yeah." (Kittering had not made *that* up, at least, Rosa Maria said to herself.) "Only thing is, I have to make sure you don't try any funny stuff while I'm showering, like calling the cops or something."

"Oh, I wouldn't do that," he said, unconvincingly.

"But a girl has to protect herself. So tonight you'll have to make the supreme sacrifice."

"Huh?"

"You'll have to give the tub a rest and take a shower." He stared at her blankly. "With me," she added.

"With *you*?"

She laughed. "Come on, it won't be so bad." She had been unzipping and unbuttoning.

"I don't know, miss . . . I've never . . ."

"There's a first time for everything, Farnsie," she said as her blouse came off. "You might even like it." She flung the blouse toward a nearby chair and stepped out of her skirt, which she hurled in the same general direction. Next she unhooked her bra, freeing her pair of eyepoppers, and tossed the bra to Farnsworth, saying, "Catch." Pantyhose were peeled down past hips, thighs, calves, toes, and dropped to the carpet.

At the sight of her lush nude body, Farnsworth's throat went dry. He appeared to be particularly mesmerized by the emphatic punctuation of her dark soft sable muff. She held out her hand. He took it. She led him into the bathroom.

As he was turned away from her, frantically pulling off his clothes, she ran her hand along the metal frame above the shower door. No key: which might have simply meant there *never* was a key, she told herself. She slid open the shower door, but before she stepped in, plucked off the black wig and hung it on the bathroom door hook. When Farnsworth, stark naked, turned around, she was a blonde.

"Hey! Your hair!" he squeaked.

"Presto, change-o."

"You're the woman who was with Field Investigator Kittering!"

"It took you long enough to tumble, Farnsie. Come on, let's do the soap-and-water number. You're not bad looking, you know? All over."

"But—"

"Later, later."

The shower was an unqualified success and evoked an enthusiastic, if largely nonverbal, response from Farnsworth that he would have found difficult to deny.

"I can tell that you liked that, Farnsie," said Rosa Maria as they dried off.

"I sure did, miss! I may take showers all the time now and give up the tub altogether."

"Oh," she said. "Listen, do you think you could stop calling me 'miss'?"

As he followed her out of the bathroom, toward his bed, he said, "I don't know your name."

"You can call me Rosie," she told him, climbing into bed and pulling him in after her.

"Rosie," he said. "I like that."

"And I like *that.*"

Farnsworth giggled. "What's your last name?" he asked.

"You don't know me *that* well," she said, engulfing him. "Not yet."

About half an hour and several galaxies later, Farnsworth whispered in Rosa Maria's ear, "Can I ask a favor of you?"

She looked at him with suspicion. "All depends."

"Well . . . I don't know quite how to say it . . . but, just for variety . . ."

Her frown of suspicion deepened. "Yeah?"

"Would you mind wearing that black wig again?"

182

She drew back. "What are you, weird?"

"I don't think so."

She fluffed her pillow-mussed yellow curls. "You don't like my real hair?"

"Sure I do," Farnsworth insisted. "I just thought it might make it a little like doing it with two different ladies."

Rosa Maria laughed good-naturedly. "You're a kinky bastard, you know that, Farnsie? Okay, why not?" She rolled out of bed and undulated into the bathroom, emerging in a moment with a head of gleaming black bangs. She said, "Maybe I'll try the wig on *you*. Only kidding, Farnsie." As she climbed back into bed, she added, "Come to think of it, though, you might look awful cute in it. Like Prince Valiant."

Rosa Maria had surpassed and surprised herself by the extent of her exertions. Farnsworth had turned out to be no wimp in bed, but a sexualist of Olympic endurance, stamina, grace, artistry, and strength; earning Rosa Maria's highest encomium, A Real Stud. Perhaps it was his youth, she told herself. For some time, she'd had only middle-aged men—Vásquez, Espinoza, Montini, Albericho, and others—plus a few men closer to her own age, like Dodd. It had been a long while since she'd balled a kid like this Farnsie, and wow, what a difference! What staying power! And did he ever have—what was that spic toast Izzy always used? *Mucho gusto!* He'd worn her out—she who was accustomed to wearing out men—and plunged her into a sleep of delicious exhaustion.

When she awoke, daylight was beginning to seep into the room, but she was alone in the bed. The kid was probably in the john, she assumed. A puckish idea tickled her funny bone. She'd call Kittering, wake her up, say 'Guess whose bed I'm calling from, got any more hot numbers in your little black book, soul sister?' She uncradled the telephone at her side, but had dialed only the first two digits when she turned her head and saw Farnsworth sitting in a chair, dressed in his shorts, looking at her appraisingly, with a smug little smile on his lips and a big gun in his hand. The phone dropped from her fingers onto the bed.

"Good morning, Rosa Maria," he said.

"Well, well, well," she muttered, reaching under the bed for her purse and razor. "Junior G-Man strikes again."

"Looking for something?" he inquired, lifting her purse into view. "Everything's here. Razor, lipstick, eyeliner, blusher, money, credit cards, passport . . . in the name of Rosa Maria Ricci. *Ricci*. Now *that's* a fine old Italian name. Where have I heard it before?"

Rosa Maria shrugged, causing her breasts to bob and quiver and register on seismographs in several adjacent counties. "So my name is Ricci. Big deal. Did I ever say it wasn't?"

"Daughter of the late Salvatore Ricci, no doubt."

"Guess again, dumbie. Sister! Daughter of the late Domenico Ricci, *Don* Domenico Ricci, 'Don Dom'—*that* was my pop, you know so much!"

"My mistake. Either way, you're one of the family. And you're in big trouble, Miss Ricci."

She laughed. "For what? Child molesting? You *look* about sixteen."

"Kidnapping a Federal agent. Use of a concealed deadly weapon."

She laughed again. "Farnsie, even *you* can't be a big enough wimp to report that! A pretty little blond lady in a black wig picked you up and took you back to your own apartment and screwed your ears off all night and you're *complaining*? Of *kidnapping*? They'd split their guts laughing at you! They'd pee in their pants! You wouldn't be able to show your face in Washington!"

But Farnsworth was unperturbed. "I'm not ashamed of

anything I've done," he said. "I acted in the best interests of the Bureau and of my country."

"And of your zucchini, too, don't forget about *that!*"

Farnsworth blushed but carried on. "I have some questions to put to you."

"Put them up your ass. I'm getting out of here." She bounced her naked body out of bed.

"Don't try it, Miss Ricci," said Farnsworth. "I'm warning you."

"Big talk from Captain Nerd. Where are my clothes?"

"In safekeeping. Please sit down."

"Fuck you, wimpo. Okay, *keep* my clothes. I don't need them. I'll walk out of here buck-ass naked." She started to do exactly that.

"You wouldn't dare."

"No? Watch me and learn something, pin-brain. In case you don't know it, Washington is a very laid-back city. A bare-ass chick walking along the street is just a who-the-fuck-*gives*-a-shit kind of thing. Someone I know did it, and I can do it, too."

Farnsworth watched with horror as she walked out of the bedroom, into the living room, straight for the front door of the apartment. *"Stop!"* he cried. "Rosie—Miss Ricci—I—"

She stopped and looked at him over her shoulder, one hand on one hip, her fine marmoreal buttocks rocking impatiently like an idling motor. "Yes?"

"I—I won't hesitate to shoot you," he said.

Her lips twisted with loathing. "You'd kill me? No way."

"No," he admitted. "I'd shoot you in the foot."

She weighed this announcement. "Yeah," she said contemptuously. "*You* would." She sat down sullenly on the nearest chair, adding "Rotten cop."

"That's better," said the shorts-clad Farnsworth, seating himself in another chair. "Now then. In your purse there's also a ticket for a chartered round-trip flight from Argentina to Washington, made out in your name, with only the first half used. The southern border of Argentina is very close to La Calavera, where Field Investigator Kittering was held prisoner. She's back in Washington now, and I've seen her with *you*, twice. Agent Dodd was sent down to La Calavera to bring her back, but he's *not* back. You asked me about a very large sum of money last night. I've had reason to suspect that Dodd ripped off a very large sum of money from your *brother*. I'd even begun to suspect that Investigator Kittering may have had a part in protecting Dodd. A jigsaw puzzle with a lot of pieces, but I can't seem to make a picture out of them. I think you can be a big help to me."

"Go f—"

Before Rosa Maria could complete her suggestion, she was interrupted. A key in the lock, a turn of the knob, and the apartment door suddenly opened. Kittering, entering, was dazed by the sight of the nude woman and the near-nude man sitting casually in the living room. The pistol in his hand seemed an almost negligible item.

"Rosa Maria! What are *you* doing here?"

"Having a party. Take off your clothes and join the fun."

"Sorry, Farnsie," said Kittering, "but you did give me a key, you know, and there are some things I've got to talk to you about—Bureau matters, among others, I've already discussed them with your chief—and I couldn't call first because it seems your phone is off the hook." She broke off and looked at Farnsworth as if studying him. "Interesting effect," she said. "Don't tell me, let me guess. Prince Valiant, right?"

Looking upward, Farnsworth blushed and quickly ripped off the black wig he'd forgotten he'd been wearing.

Then Rosa Maria sprang from her chair like a naked jack-in-the-box, kicked the gun out of Farnsworth's hand with a bare heel, and scooped it into her own hand before he, in his open-jawed embarrassment, knew what was happening.

She leaped behind his chair and jammed the pistol into the back of his head, while with her free arm she jack-knifed his larynx until he gagged.

In a chain-saw voice she ordered Kittering to "Drop the purse, honey—*now!*" Kittering obeyed. "Now listen. No more jerking me around. I'm going to ask you a question, *just once.* Then I'm going to count to three. If you haven't given me a straight answer by the time I get to three, I turn his brains into Hamburger Helper. Capeesh? Now here's the question. Where. Is. The. Fucking. MONEY! One . . . two . . ."

Part

VI

24

"HOW will we locate the ladies, Señor Dodd?" Dodd and Vásquez were on the last leg of their chartered flight to Washington. Vásquez was drinking a plastic tumbler of Royal Crown Cola with a twist of lemon. Dodd was nursing straight gin on the rocks.

"Shouldn't be too hard, Presidente. Kittering's apartment will have to be checked out first. Don't worry, we'll find them. I'm an FBI man, remember?"

"I do not trust you."

"Why not?"

"You are an FBI man, remember?"

"But I'm working for *you!*" Dodd reminded him.

Vásquez moaned and put down his cola. "Everything was so beautiful. I was wealthy, successful, secure, a head of state, lord of all I surveyed. I was married to a passionate woman with the body of a goddess. What man could desire more? Then Salvatore Ricci was killed. From that day, my troubles began to multiply. And all of them were spelled D-O-D."

"That's D-O-*D*-D," said Dodd. "D-O-D means Dead On Delivery."

El Presidente's eyes flashed. "Ah!" he snarled. "That was my first mistake! Letting you live when you landed on La Calavera. I should have killed you at once! Dead On Delivery! That ridiculous disguise . . . dressed in

Salvatore's clothes . . . the same clothes you are wearing now . . . do you really think you will deceive the Customs inspector looking like that?"

Dodd shrugged. "It fooled *you*," he said.

"From a distance! And only for a moment! But the Customs man will be *this close* to you!" Vásquez thrust his face into Dodd's.

"I'll wing it."

Vásquez laughed. "I am glad I will be there to observe this winging! It will be most amusing to see you exposed, embarrassed, taken into custody, perhaps!"

"Hey, don't get *too* amused, Presidente," Dodd advised him. "Without me, how are you going to find Mrs. V?"

"I am not exactly an imbecile," said Vásquez. "I have . . . conniptions? . . ."

"Connections. Yeah, I'm sure you have. But who with?"

"My American partners. Members of the Señora's own people, her own family. They are not without resources."

It was Dodd's turn to laugh. "I can just see you trying to explain to the Mafia why you're looking for her, what she's doing here. What the hell are you going to tell them?"

"I—I will wing it," said Vásquez as the two passengers were advised to fasten their seat belts and observe the NO SMOKING sign.

Dodd was glad to be back in the land of his birth. Even Dulles International Airport looked good to him, smelled good, felt good under his feet. Happy anticipation of Kittering's bed and the four hundred thousand dollars augmented the good feeling.

"After you, Presidente," he said, graciously waving Vásquez ahead of himself in the Customs line-up.

"No, no," responded Vásquez with a chuckle. "You first. I would not miss this for all the tea in England!"

"China," said Dodd. "Okay, if you insist." Dodd stepped forward and presented the Ricci passport.

The Customs inspector peered at the passport photo, then at Dodd. "Salvatore Ricci?" he asked.

Dodd nodded.

"Would you please remove the dark glasses, sir?"

Dodd, blinking, pulled off Ricci's famous wraparounds.

"And the hat, please?"

Off came the Borsalino.

"And the wig?"

Vásquez suppressed a guffaw.

"Sure thing," said Dodd. "Actually, I'm not Salvatore Ricci. I'm an FBI agent, working undercover . . ."

"Really, sir?" said the Customs man in a bored yet menacing tone.

"Yeah, see?" Dodd yanked off the gray wig and peeled his FBI I.D. from the lining to which it had been taped. He handed it to the Customs man, who examined it carefully, taking his time.

Finally the inspector returned the I.D. and the passport. "Thank you, Agent Dodd," he said. "Have a nice day."

"I sure will. Thanks a bunch." Dodd moved forward, allowing Vásquez to take his place.

El Presidente produced his passport with a flourish and presented it.

"You're Ysidro Vásquez Gutiérrez?" the Customs man inquired.

"That is correct."

"The man in this photograph is wearing an eyepatch, sir."

Vásquez smiled. "I have since replaced it with an eye of glass." He tapped it with a fingernail, tink-tink.

"I see. Will you please accompany these officers, Mr. Gutiérrez?"

"Vásquez," said Vásquez. "What officers?" His question was answered by large hands firmly grasping both of his arms.

"I protest!" he protested.

As he was unceremoniously hustled behind the scenes, Vásquez screamed, "I am the President of La Calavera! I am a head of state! *I have diplomatic immunity!*"

"You have a big mouth, too, creepo," said the biggest of the officers.

The last thing Vásquez saw before he vanished into the nightmare of strip searching and endless interrogation was Dodd, kissing his fingers to him in farewell.

"Ga-gla-gla-ga-gla . . ." Farnsworth seemed to be saying through his crushed throat, held in the vise of Rosa Maria's arm.

". . . *Three!*" cried Rosa Maria, bare as birth, pressing Farnsworth's own pistol into the back of his head.

"Hold it," said Kittering, with appropriate gestures of surrender.

"Okay, talk!"

"Ease up on him first, will you? Before you strangle him?"

The Sicilian spitfire relaxed her hold on Farnsworth, and he gratefully gasped for air.

Kittering shook her head. "If you only knew how silly the two of you look. Naked, half naked, waving a piece. Why don't you put it down, Rosa Maria?"

"Not a chance. He was waving another kind of piece all night, lover-boy here, softening me up."

"That's not true, Rosie!" Farnsworth insisted. "It wasn't until this morning—"

She ignored him. "And I was dumb enough to fall for it. To fall for *him*. I should have known better than to trust a cop. I'll never trust one again—including *you*, bunkie. Quit the stall or I blow his seeds off and then start in on you."

"Right," said Kittering. "You've got it. But all I can tell you is where the money *should* be. Whether it's there or not probably only Farnsie can tell us."

"*Me?*" croaked Farnsworth, rubbing his throat.

"Keep talking," said Rosa Maria.

"The money should be where I told you it was all along, in my p.o. box. On the other hand, the key to that box *should* be taped to the top of Farnsie's shower door—but it isn't. So I wouldn't be surprised if the money's missing, too."

"That key is *yours?*" yelped Farnsworth.

"Yes!" said Kittering. "Where's the money?"

"WHAT MONEY?"

Both Kittering and Rosa Maria groaned.

Farnsworth added, "I don't know anything about any money!"

"Then what did you do with that damn key?" Rosa Maria demanded. "Stick it in your ass?"

"*I* didn't find it," Farnsworth told Kittering. "The Chief did. *He* opened the p.o. box."

"Then the *Chief* has the money?"

"No, no. There was a package of top-secret blueprints in your p.o. box—ICBM stuff, very sensitive."

"*What?*"

"But they weren't addressed to your box number. It was another number, one digit off. The postal clerk made a mistake." Then Farnsworth snapped his fingers in chagrin and said, "Oh, *shoot!*"

It was the first time Kittering had heard him use such strong language. "What's the matter?" she asked.

"I wasn't supposed to tell anybody that. It was supposed to be only between me and the Chief. He told the Director a different version."

"Why?"

"For his own good. Mine, too. The truth is, he walked all over my Constitutional rights when he entered and searched my apartment without my knowledge and without a warrant. So he told the Director *I* found the key in my own shower—left there by a former tenant—and I got a promotion for uncovering an espionage plot."

"It couldn't have happened to a nicer guy," said Kittering.

"Wait a minute, *wait a minute!*" wailed Rosa Maria. "You guys are making me crazy."

"Wouldn't you like to get some clothes on?" Kittering suggested.

"And drop the cannon? And watch you two run out of here while I'm hooking my bra? Forget it. Everything stays just like it is, until we untangle some of the kinks."

Rosa Maria had bobbed out nimbly from behind Farnsworth's chair, keeping a firm grip on the pistol, and tiptoed daintily if bouncingly across to an immense ottoman, where she now perched, legs crossed, hands poised on her knee. Farnsworth, notwithstanding his recent brush with death by strangulation, couldn't keep his eyes off her.

"I think you're exciting Farnsie," said Kittering.

"Down, boy," Rosa Maria muttered scornfully.

"Sorry," he murmured, attempting to cup in his hands a rapidly expanding bulge under his Fruit of the Loom. Recovering quickly from his embarrassment, if not from his excitement, he said smugly to Kittering, "So I was right, after all, about that money and Dodd's deposit box."

"No," she snapped, "you were *not* right. 'That money' has nothing to do with Dodd's deposit box. The only thing Dodd kept in the box was a Bible. The money under discussion is Justice Department property."

"Ricci family property!" Rosa Maria interrupted.

"Then why," Farnsworth asked, "should it be in your personal p.o. box, if it's Department property?"

"That's really none of your business, Farnsie, but if you really think you deserve an explanation, it's being used to bait a hook to catch other fish. It happens to be marked money, easily identified if you know how. Right, Rosa Maria?"

Rosa Maria nodded sullenly, her grip on the gun slackening.

"And why—" Farnsworth started to ask.

But Kittering cut him off: "That's all you get."

"I just wanted to ask why you were talking to my Chief. When you walked in here, you said you had talked to him."

"Oh, that. Well, I decided it was no longer useful to be undercover—particularly after you spotted me in that coffeeshop—so I decided to check in to the Justice Department, turn in my report of the whole La Calavera affair, and then inform Dodd's Chief that Dodd was still down there, trying to get him*self* out. As you can see, he managed to get me out pretty neatly. That's when I found out that you and your boys were staking out my digs, so I thought I'd better drop over and let you know you could call off the dogs. I even thought we might work in a quickie before you punched in at the Bureau, but I see that your heart belongs to another."

"You can *have* this turkey," Rosa Maria said without conviction.

Then, in a mixture of awe and admiration, she said, "Kittering, you bitch, you did it again. I gave you to the count of three to tell me where that money is, and I counted all the way to three, and I didn't blow his brains out, and you talked my ass off, but I *still* don't have an answer! I don't believe it. I don't fucking *believe* it!"

Kittering sighed. "Rosa Maria, haven't you been paying attention? I don't know where the money is. Farnsie doesn't know where the money is. Listen very closely. *Nobody knows where the money is.*"

25

HE had a head like a shoe box: rectangular, flat-faced, utilitarian, and uninteresting. In fact, he looked as if he was constructed entirely of boxes—a large packing case for a torso; long, jointed flower boxes for arms and legs. This was in spite of the high-quality suit from Brooks Brothers, and was probably due to the fact that he felt a stranger in it, the suit was wearing him.

He opened the p.o. box, pulled out the hefty package inside, locked the box again, and quickly slipped the package into his commodious briefcase. Then he walked purposefully out of the Georgetown post office.

He waited until he was a block away before hailing a cab. Climbing in, he told the driver in a quiet voice to take him to 1119 16th Street. As the cab moved, he sat stiffly, with the briefcase on his lap. After a moment he removed his hat and ran a hand over the thick hair that was brushed straight back from his forehead without a part. It was warm here in Washington, sometimes a bit too warm. But he liked the warmth.

The driver headed up 16th Street, past the Sheraton-Carlton and Capitol Hilton hotels, and pulled up in front of 1119. "Oh, *this* place," he said. "Why didn't you say so?"

His passenger knew the exact fare because he had made this same trip—to the precise inch—many times, and he paid it plus a generous tip. He got out, tightening his grasp on the briefcase, and walked toward the main entrance of the palatial mansion. It had been built during the administration of President Taft by Mrs. George M. Pullman, widow of the noted sleeping-car magnate, and was an imposing monument not only to him but to the undaunted spirit of American capitalism. Currently it served as the Soviet Embassy.

As he entered, a young man at a reception desk looked up and greeted him in Russian: "Good day, Comrade Arensky." Arensky nodded curtly to the KGB bastard and walked on, down stately halls, past magnificently appointed offices, until he came at last to the relatively remote, decidedly small, and sparsely furnished office that had been allotted to him.

Kiril Maksimovich Arensky was a minor functionary attached to the Embassy. His work was unimportant and routine. It demanded few skills, little training, and no talent. The pay was minimal. That didn't matter to him. The real pay was *Washington*. He loved Washington. He loved everything about it. The restaurants, the theaters, the parks, the climate, the free and easy way the people thought and talked and the wine flowed and the girls walked . . . one girl in particular. He smiled, thinking of her.

Yes, Washington was a plum of a posting. His wife, Natasha, liked it, too. Kiril Maksimovich loved his wife, of course, and what she didn't know wouldn't hurt her, but his affection for the enticing Cindy was of another order. What an adorable little minx she was! So engagingly decadent! So American, in all the best and the worst ways! He liked her worst ways best of all! "Cindy, accent on the first syllable," he'd said to her playfully once, but she hadn't comprehended the joke until he'd explained it to her. What did that matter? What did he care if she was not a member of the intelligentsia and was only a dear little switchboard operator at the Capitol Hilton Hotel? He had never known anyone like her: not in his native Smolensk, not in Moscow, not even in Leningrad.

He entered his tiny office, locked the door, and placed his briefcase carefully upon the desk. He hung up his hat. He sat behind the desk and drummed his fingers on the briefcase, humming a Bruce Springsteen tune that was a favorite of Cindy's. It was because of the contents of this briefcase, he reminded himself, that he had been permitted to stay in Washington far longer than the usual tour of duty. Others, many others, had been replaced, repatriated; he had seen them come and (weeping) go; but he had outstayed them all. That was because he performed special duties for Moscow, above and beyond the call of routine.

He opened the briefcase. The plain brown package was face down in the case, its blank side toward him. He lifted it out and turned it over.

And went cold, despite the Washington heat.

An animal instinct made him glance fearfully over his shoulder, even though he knew there was no one else in the locked office, and it was free of closed circuit TV cameras—he had made sure of that. But he had lived for too many years in a society choked by the weeds of betrayal, deception, and duplicity, and its habits had stamped themselves into the inmost fibers of his nerves. He looked again at the package.

What horror was this? What infamous error—or trickery? His mouth went dry, his palms became slick. The package was of the usual size and sort—a bit thicker, perhaps—and marked BOOKS, according to plan, and bore no return . . . all standard procedure. But it was misaddressed! Instead of the proper addressee, which should have been the nonexistent Utility Services Supply Registrar, this package was addressed to a woman! A woman named Sally Rich.

Sally Rich? Who in the sacred names of Marx, Engels, Lenin, and the Central Committee was Sally Rich?

He peered more closely at the p.o. box number and realized that it was just one digit higher than his own. He shouted vile curses in his native tongue. Some stupid postal clerk had simply put this package in the wrong box—in his box. But where was *his* package?

He gulped and went even colder. In Sally Rich's p.o. box?

He groaned. Typical democratic inefficiency! In the Soviet, such slovenly work would be severely punished. Here the idiot probably would receive periodic promotions and a pension.

What was to be done?

He must return this package to the post office at once, report the error, and demand to see the mail that had been delivered to this Sally Rich's p.o. box.

No. That was much too dangerous. It would lead to questions, investigations . . . it would call attention to himself and to the fact that he had a p.o. box, in itself suspicious.

In a frenzy, he searched the pages of the telephone directory for a Sally Rich. There was no listing for such a person. Of course not. Why should there be? There was no listing for United Services Supply Registrar, either.

His heart fell into his stomach, his stomach turned upside down. This was the end of him. If he failed to provide those blueprints—the most important of all the blueprints and other papers that he had procured for his masters over the years—he would be recalled at once. Back to the Soviet. No more Washington. No more Cindy. Not only that—he would be punished. Put under suspicion. Interrogated to within an inch of his life. And then . . . what? Lubyanka Prison? A bullet in the back of the head? Perhaps, if he was lucky. If he was not lucky, an endless sentence to hard labor and starvation diet in the Arctic reaches of the Gulag.

One careless mistake by a postal employee and his life was destroyed.

He felt as if he were going to faint. After opening the deep side drawer of his desk, he took out an almost depleted bottle of Stolichnaya vodka and gulped down a mighty jolt. The bottle was empty when he put it back in the drawer.

The potent liquor calmed him. Perhaps all was not lost. He could return this package to the post office by simply dropping it into any convenient mail box. And he would hope that Sally Rich, when she opened her p.o. box and saw a package not intended for her, would also return it. Hope, that was the word. He must continue to hope. And—yes, why not?—and pray. His mother had been a devout member of the Orthodox Church and had named him after St. Cyril, who brought Russia the word of Christ and the alphabet. Yes, Kiril Maksimovich told himself, why not pray?

Now he looked at the package again. Who was this Sally Rich? he wondered. Some silly shopgirl? A *petite bourgeoise* housewife? A dotty D.A.R. dowager?

What sort of books were these? Trashy romantic novels? Boring religious tracts? Vicious anti-Communist propaganda? It might be useful to know. The package was stapled shut at one end by just a half dozen or so thin wire staples. He could extract them easily, with the little staple remover on his desk, then close up the package again with his own stapler. Nothing could be simpler.

He proceeded to do so, carefully prying the staples out, one by one, with the metal jaws of his staple remover, until the package gaped open at one end. Tipping it, he shook the contents out upon his desk.

His eyes bulged. *"Bozhemoi!"* he whispered.

A small mountain of money stood before his awestruck

gaze. Slowly he began to count it. When he was finished, he whispered "My God!" again—this time in English, for some reason, perhaps out of respect for the American currency. "Four . . . hundred . . . thousand . . . dollars!"

His shoe box face broadened with an ecstatic smile. "Cindy!" he said. "This is our ticket to Paradise! Or, at the very least, to Rio de Janeiro!"

26

"CAN I have my piece back now, Rosie? Please?"
Rosa Maria, poised nude on the ottoman, considered the request. "Oh, all right," she said. "Catch."

She tossed it to Farnsworth underhand. Off guard, he fumbled, and the pistol thumped to the carpet. He reached down and retrieved it.

"And now," she said, "if you'll tell me where you've hidden my clothes, I'll get dressed."

Kittering giggled. "Did you really hide her clothes, Farnsie?"

"In the dresser," he replied, pointing toward the bedroom. "Third drawer from the top."

Rosa Maria jumped up from the ottoman and jounced into the bedroom. "Back in a flash," she said.

Farnsworth looked down at his near-naked self. "Guess I'd better get dressed, too."

"Later," Kittering whispered, moving closer to him. "Listen, Farnsie, it was a stroke of luck finding Rosa Maria here, because the Bureau wants to talk to her and was hoping I'd bring her in. But don't you think it would be better if you'd do that? It would look good on your record."

"Maybe it would, but why do they want her? What has she done? What's the charge?"

"No charge. She hasn't done anything. They just want

to ask her some questions, pick her brains, pump her, whatever you want to call it. After all, she's the sister of Big Sal Ricci and the wife of Vásquez, the biggest cocaine pusher in the world. She could be a big help. They'll never have an opportunity like this again."

"Can they force her?"

Kittering shrugged. "They can and they can't. They can drag her in and hold her for a while 'on suspicion' of this or that, and then release her. But while they've got her, they could get a lot out of her—maybe a lot about why she was sitting around naked in your apartment . . ."

"Now, wait a minute . . ."

"Unless *you* bring her in, and prepare them for a lot of wild sexual fantasies and slanders she threatened you with if you turned her over to them."

Farnsworth nodded slowly.

Kittering said, "Let me slip into the bedroom and talk to her, keep her occupied for a minute or two while you get on the phone to the Bureau and get some backup over here."

"I don't need any backup to handle a woman!"

"Are you sure?"

Indignantly he replied, "Of course I'm sure!"

"Well, at least I'm here, if you need help."

Farnsworth stood up. "I'd rather you left," he said with as much dignity as he could summon in his shorts. "But . . . I do thank you for your suggestions."

"You're welcome, Farnsie," said Kittering, heading for the door. "Good luck with Rosa Maria. She's a spicy meatball."

Kittering was returning from her kitchen to her bedroom, clad only in Dodd's shirt, spooning up something from a little dish.

"Sure you don't want any of this frozen tofu dessert?" she asked. "It's awfully good."

"No, thanks, I'm fine," said Dodd from her bed.

"You know," she said, "in a way, I'm a little sorry about Vásquez. He was kind of charming."

Dodd was profoundly shocked. "You're not shedding any tears over *him*, are you? The guy who chopped off your finger? How is it, by the way?"

"Coming along nicely." She held up her slightly foreshortened left pinkie, its only dressing now a small Band-Aid. "Even this should be coming off soon. The doctor tells me wonderful prosthetic fingertips are available now that look like the real thing, complete with nails that take polish. Fun at cocktail parties, huh? Pull it off and scratch my ear with it? Great conversation piece?"

"Or conversation stopper," said Dodd. "Tell me about Rosa. What's she been up to?"

"I don't want to talk about your other girls. Tell you later. You wouldn't believe it, anyway. Don't you want to hear about the money?"

"Let's talk about the money."

She gave him a quick rundown, winding up by saying, "So actually, everything turned out fine, if not exactly the way I planned it."

Dodd exploded. " *'Fine'?!* My four hundred G's—all right, *our* four hundred G's—just *vanishes*, and you say it's *fine?*"

She leaned over and kissed his nose. "Dodd, it wasn't yours, it wasn't ours, it wasn't Ricci's. I guess it was the property of the Justice Department, or Internal Revenue—technically, anyway. But the money really belonged to all those poor suckers who lost it at Ricci's casinos. And the money didn't vanish. *Some*body's got it. It really doesn't matter who—as long as it isn't you."

"What??"

"Don't get upset." She kissed his cheek. "Did you really think I saved you from the long nose of Farnsie just to split the swag with you? Be your partner in crime?"

"Sure. Why not? Made perfect sense."

"Perfect nonsense. And no moral sense. But that's you, Dodd. No moral sense at all. You're the most amoral person I've ever known. I mean, you're not *evil*, like Ricci or Fontana, you're a sweet guy and I love you, but you're a complete pagan. I had to save you—not just from Farnsie, that was easy, but from yourself. That was a little harder."

"Thanks a *lot*," Dodd said acidly.

"You're very welcome. If I hadn't, you'd have landed yourself in the Federal slammer. So I pretended to throw in with you. And I stashed the money, planning to donate it anonymously to some worthy charity and then let you down easily. It didn't work out quite that way, but almost."

Spluttering with exasperation, Dodd said, "But why, *why* did you hide the key in Farnsie's shower? That was so . . . God . . . damn . . . *dumb!*"

"It seemed like a good idea at the time," she replied. "Farnsie isn't quite as stupid as he looks, and I had a hunch he suspected I'd had something to do with that deposit box switch. I was afraid he might search my place and find the key. I had to hide it where he'd never think of looking. It worked—until, for some reason I *still* don't understand, your chief decided to search Farnsie's apartment! Any more questions?"

"Just one," said Dodd. "I'm the most amoral person you've ever known?"

"Uh-huh. No offense intended."

"None taken. But what about yourself, sweetass? What do you call a lady who bangs a flea-head like Farnsworth just so she can hide a key in his apartment?"

"*Not* just for that. He asked me for a date, and I said yes because I found him attractive. Incidentally, he turned out to be terrific in the sack."

"Loud cheers. But talk about amoral! . . ."

Kittering shook her head. "*Im*moral," she said. "Totally different. Filthy, disgusting, depraved. Like this . . ."

The Chief sat behind his huge cold tombstone of a desk, looking at Dodd, who was standing more or less at attention before him, dressed again in one of his fine suits from Arthur Adler's. Dodd felt that some of the faces in the Chief's gallery had grown more menacing during his absence: Woodrow Wilson and Truman Capote seemed to glare at him with especial malice. On the other hand, Bearcat Stutz, king of the big-time gamblers, appeared to beam beatifically upon him.

"Welcome home," the Chief said in an emotionless voice. "It's good to see you." He added, with some surprise, "I never thought I'd say that to you, Dodd. Sit down."

Dodd sat, saying, "Thanks, Chief. Good to be back."

"The Director is very pleased with your extrication of Field Investigator Kittering from the clutches of the vile Vásquez."

"I know. He told me."

"He also admires the way you delivered the aforesaid Vásquez into the hands of the law, from whence he shall not soon escape, I assure you, particularly after we extract damning testimony from his wife."

"But a wife can't be forced to—"

"Force?" said the Chief with great innocence. "We will not *force* her. She will be persuaded to cooperate, for the sake of the Greater Good."

"Oh," said Dodd.

The Chief fingered a file folder that lay open before him on the massive desk. "I've been studying your report," he said. "Very detailed, very professional. But what I fail to understand is why that fool Vásquez entered the country with cocaine concealed on his person. In an inkwell, of all things. . . ."

208

"Do you really want to know, Chief?" Dodd inquired.

"Strangely enough, I do, although I shall probably have cause to regret my curiosity."

"I planted it on him," said Dodd. The Chief closed his eyes in martyrdom. "That was sort of my scheme from the time I first learned that the little Chinese inkwell had the stuff in it. But then this Camorra fellow showed up— Davioni, I mentioned him in the report?—and I had to tell him it was the opera singer's ashes to get *him* off our backs, so then I had to lift it from him and slip it into El Presidente's pocket just before we landed at Dulles. Our upside-down landing in Argentina was a help. A lot of stuff fell out of all our pockets, and it was easier to make the switch. Not easy, but easier. And I had a little note for the Customs man all ready, folded up with my I.D. inside the wig. Did that before we left La Calavera, of course."

"Note?" asked the Chief. "Wig?"

"The wig I wore to pass for Ricci. I kept my FBI I.D. taped to the lining. The note just said, *This man Vásquez is carrying concealed drugs. Search him and contact the Justice Department.*"

The Chief sighed. "As usual, I find your methods somewhat unorthodox for my taste, but possibly I'm old-fashioned. We will keep this conversation off the record, of course."

Dodd thought it best to say nothing.

"I hope," the Chief continued, "that you didn't resent being sent to the back of beyond on such a bizarre mission?"

"Not at all," replied Dodd. "A nice change."

"And you have had sufficient time to recover from the rigors of that assignment? All rested, are you?"

"Bright-tailed and bushy-eyed, Chief."

"Excellent. Then, seeing that you're fit for work, I know you won't mind if I send you out of the country again."

"Really, Chief? So soon?" Dodd's face had fallen.

"No place exotic, nothing dangerous. Just bring back somebody from Canada."

"Oh. Extradition. Who's the culprit?"

"It's not an official extradition proceeding," said the Chief. "More in the nature of an informal, er, escort service. The culprit is Rosa Maria Vásquez, *née* Ricci."

Dodd blinked. "Rosa? In Canada? What's she doing *there*? And, if you don't mind my asking, Chief, why am I being sent on an errand boy's job when I'm a Supervisory Special Agent?"

"So many questions! My, my!" The Chief sat back in his chair. "I *do* mind your asking, Dodd. Yours not to reason why. However, I'm feeling magnanimous this morning, so I'll answer your questions. Originally, we merely wanted to ask Señora Vásquez a few things about her husband's and her brother's criminal activities. There were no charges against her. But now there are, I'm afraid, because she has kidnapped an agent of this Bureau at the point of his own service pistol and forced him to drive her over the Canadian border."

Dodd held up one hand. "Wait. Don't tell me. Farnsworth."

"Of course."

"Have you had a ransom note from her?"

"No," the Chief said with another great sigh. "I received what I suppose we might call a ransom phone call—from Farnsworth. He told me that if we will agree to drop the kidnapping charge and forget about questioning her in regard to Vásquez and Ricci, he knows he will have no difficulty persuading Mrs. Farnsworth to return with him."

Dodd shot forward in his chair. "Mrs. *who?*"

"It seems that they were married in Canada, and are, in point of fact, passionately in love with one another."

"But—but—for one thing—that's bigamy!"

"A mere detail," the Chief assured him.

"But," Dodd persisted, "why do you want to bother about those two? Let them stay up there. Do you really need her for questioning? Do you really need *him?* For *anything?*"

The Chief nodded. "Unfortunately, I do. The Director thinks very highly of him because of some blueprints the boy brilliantly uncovered—"

"Yeah, I heard all about his 'brilliance'!"

"—And if the Director were to learn that Farnsworth had been abducted to Canada by a woman—whom he then *married*—and that this woman is the sister of Ricci and the wife of Vásquez . . . I'm afraid he would be terribly unhappy. The ripples of his unhappiness would be felt throughout the Bureau. For our own peace of mind—and job security—it behooves us to keep our Director happy."

Dodd nodded glumly.

"That's why we must *sever* this so-called marriage!" shouted the Chief, bringing the side of his hand down on his desk like a guillotine blade. "Someone with ingenuity and the gift of gab must go up there and talk Farnsworth out of it, destroy all legal records of it, and bring that sex-besotted idiot back to his senses and back to Washington."

"What about Rosa?"

"Bring her back, too. After we sweat a few pounds off her voluptuous figure in our interrogation rooms, we'll deport her as an undesirable alien."

"You can't do that! She's a U.S. citizen!"

"Aha!" cried the Chief, with the carnivorous grin of Tyrannosaurus Rex. "Not any more she isn't! When she married President Vásquez and became his First Lady, she signed a marriage contract that, among other things, dissolved past national allegiances, making her a citizen of La Calavera—and *that's* where we will send her."

"Chief, I've got to hand it to you," Dodd said with

unfeigned admiration. "You are a real genuine hickory-smoked son of a bitch."

The Chief blushed modestly. "All in a day's work, my dear fellow. Here's your airline ticket and a memorandum of particulars. Have a nice trip."

Glancing at the ticket as he left the Chief's office, Dodd smiled grimly.

He was able to manage a stopover in New York to see his mother, whom he hadn't visited in years.

"Kiddo!" she shrieked when she opened her apartment door. "You got older!"

"You got younger, Ma."

They embraced, and she said, "Come on in, meet my new main squeeze. Hey, Dee-Dee? . . . oh, I guess he's in the shower. He'll be out in a minute. When I told him my son was coming over, he said I didn't look old enough to have a grown son. How's that for road apples, huh? I love it, though. I didn't tell him you're a Fed—that throws a scare into some people, know what I mean? Oh, but he's a wonderful guy, kiddo."

Mrs. Rudnick's small apartment was a cozy clutter of mementoes from several past decades and marriages: a tall green glass bottle from the Fifties, a lava lamp from the Sixties, an ocean-in-a-bottle from the Seventies, and other nostalgic junk, some of which sent sweet-and-sour twinges from his childhood flashing through Dodd's heart.

"Will you be able to stick around for a few days?" his mother wanted to know.

"Just passing through on my way to Halifax."

"I had to ask! You'll love this guy. He's going to make me rich."

Dodd was alerted. "Hey, Ma, you're not giving him your savings to invest, are you?"

"Hell, no! I've still got all my marbles! I won a bundle in

Vegas. He showed me how. We just got back. Had a great time. You were there not so long ago, right?"

Nodding, Dodd asked, "What do you mean, he showed you how?"

"Then we went to Reno. But before that, we knocked over a lot of places closer by, in Atlantic City."

"'Knocked over'?"

"The slot machines. They're electric. Well, Dee-Dee wrapped an automobile coil around my waist, under my dress—perfectly safe, all insulated and everything—and showed me just how and when to give those machines a forty-thousand-volt blast and knock free a jackpot. *Zammo!* It works like a charm!"

Dodd groaned.

"Meanwhile," his mother continued, "Dee-Dee is working another row of slots with his magnet."

"Magnet?"

"Yep, he palms it and just slaps it on the side of the machine to freeze the mechanism. Works almost as good as the auto coil."

"Ma, Ma, *Ma!* That's illegal!"

"The magnet?"

"The magnet, the coil, all of it!"

"It is?" she said innocently. "But those places bleed folks dry, don't they? I thought the whole idea was we were supposed to pit our wits against theirs and take them any way we can."

"Not that way. Believe me. You've got to stop, Ma, or you'll end up in jail, you and this . . . Dee-Dee . . ."

"Gee, all right, if you say so," she said, disappointed. "But we were just getting started. Too bad. We were going to quit when we piled up two hundred grand—we're not greedy—but now we'll never see that dream come true."

"And a good thing, too. How much did you make, all told?"

"Well, we've only been at it a few days. A hundred and eighty-nine thousand and change."

"*What?*"

"Of course, I had to split it fifty-fifty with him. Listen, kiddo, should I declare it on my income tax form?"

"*No!*"

"No? Well, anything you say." She beckoned Dodd to bend down so she could whisper in his ear. "Don't say anything to him about this, okay? I'll break it to him easy, later on. And don't let's tell him you're a Fed."

"Okay, Ma."

A man with gray hair and wet bare feet, wearing one of Mrs. Rudnick's bathrobes, entered the room.

"Dee-Dee," said Mrs. Rudnick, "this is my bouncing baby boy. Kiddo, this is Dee-Dee."

"Nice to meet you," Dodd murmured in a daze, instantly recognizing his mother's new friend.

"Likewise," said D. D. ("Bearcat") Stutz.

"Well, I've got a plane to catch," Dodd mumbled. "Duty calls, and all that. So long, Ma, I'll be in touch. Good-bye, Mr. . . . uh . . . Dee-Dee . . ."

At Kennedy, Dodd made one long-distance phone call before boarding his plane. It was to the Chief, informing him of the whereabouts of the wanted Bearcat Stutz and demanding that his mother be spared the slightest hint of danger, embarrassment, and even knowledge of Bearcat's arrest.

"Thy will be done," the Chief promised him.

In the air again, Dodd settled himself into his seat and let lassitude cover him like a heavy quilt.

What would he say to Farnsworth? He'd worry about that later. He'd wing it. Maybe he wouldn't have to say much of anything. Maybe Farnsie would do all the talking. Maybe Rosa would. Or maybe Rosa would ventilate him with Farnsie's faithful service pistol. By now her doting bridegroom must have told her all about nasty Dodd being the one who'd iced her brother. Hell, maybe the plane would go down and he'd never even *get* to Canada, solving all his problems.

The strain of recent events took its toll. Dodd closed his eyes and, dreaming of Kittering's pearly pelt, slept all the way to Nova Scotia.